# THE CURIOUS CASE OF DR. PRAGYAN PARKER

## UNHEARD STORIES OF SCIENCE & THE SCIENTISTS

**STORYTELLER SCIENTIST**

INDIA • SINGAPORE • MALAYSIA

ISBN  979-8-89322-958-5

# DISCLAIMER

This book is a work of semi-fiction, blending factual scientific information with a fictional narrative to educate and entertain. While it discusses the mechanisms of action of various medicines and explores concepts in chemistry and biology, it is not intended as a substitute for professional medical advice, diagnosis, or treatment. The scientific content has been carefully researched and presented with educational intentions; however, readers should consult a qualified healthcare provider for health-related questions or concerns.

The names of prescription medicines and their uses mentioned in this book are based on real medications and scientific principles. However, the context in which they are presented is part of a fictional storyline and should not be taken as guidance for medication use. The author and publisher strongly advise against the use of any prescription medicine without the direction of a licensed medical professional.

This book is designed to engage and inform a general audience, particularly appealing to school students under parental discretion. Parents and guardians are encouraged to review the content of this book to determine its appropriateness for their children's reading material. While the book aims to foster an interest in science and medicine among readers of all ages, it recognises the importance of guidance for young readers engaging with complex or sensitive subjects.

Any resemblance of names, characters, or events to actual persons, living or dead, or real events is purely coincidental. By reading this book, you acknowledge and agree that the author and publisher are not responsible for any misconceptions, medical decisions, or actions taken by readers based on the content herein. The narrative is intended to inspire curiosity and learning in chemistry and biology. It should be enjoyed as a journey into the vast world of science, woven into a tale of mystery and determination.

Enjoy your adventure into science and story and remember that knowledge is most valuable when accompanied by wisdom.

What if I told you scientists are trying to make strong painkillers from snake and scorpion poison?

Call it a curse or a gift; there is a family in Italy that does not feel pain due to some defect in their genes.

If that's not enough, a parasite infects mice and plays with their mind. The infection makes mice lose their fear towards cats. The result: Mice indulge in risky behaviours and are eaten up quickly during a cat's brunch.

Why does a flower try to look and smell like rotten meat?

Do plants and bacteria have a social network, and if so, what do they use it for?

Did you know certain plants hire insect assassins to kill the herbivores partying on their leaves?

What are mother trees, and why are they called so? Do plants have memory? Can they be labelled as intelligent?

Science is full of intriguing stories like these, which sometimes do not reach students. These stories are the greatest testament to the beauty and awe of science and are also the best way to introduce the subject to students.

As an educator, I had firsthand experience of the pain students endured while learning science. It was a wish to create something that would ease their burden and make them fall in love with the subject's beauty. Being a massive fan of Sherlock Holmes, I devised a mystery-driven narrative and made the subject matter as fun and engaging as possible.

I am sure you will enjoy this book. Every single second spent completing it would be worth it if even one of you feels the awe of science.

# Acknowledgements

There are some incredible people who helped me along this journey. I am indebted to the support of Vijay Sindha, Pratyush Sarin, Amritansh Mehrotra, Pakshal Shah and my students who read the initial drafts.

**2.30 PM, Prime Minister's office.**

"Dr. Parker, the honourable prime minister, would now see you," said an officer in his forties.

"Hello, Dr. Parker, the learning methodology and content you have developed will be a game-changer for the nation. The government will extend all its support for executing your education programme. However, you are responsible for ensuring that the methodology and the system remain a top secret for some years. This is non-negotiable. I hope I am clear on this," said the prime minister.

"Sure, sir. For me, nothing comes before my country. Come what may, I will ensure that this stays between you and me until your next order and the success of our mission. It is my dream to make our kids fall in eternal love with science. I am on a mission to train an army of scientists and technocrats who will use science to serve society," said Dr. Parker.

**6.30 PM, Vigyan Villa, Dr. Parker's residence.**

"Hello, Am I talking to Dr. Parker?"

"Yes, Dr. Parker speaking."

"We have kidnapped your son."

"What? I hope this is not a prank call."

"Of course not; please check your WhatsApp immediately."

Dr. Parker pressed the red icon to end the call. Never in his life had he been so afraid of a WhatsApp notification. His WhatsApp wallpaper had Stephen Hawking's equation of black hole entropy. These tiny alphabets within the equations have often conveyed some of the greatest truths of the universe in the most compact manner possible. Sometimes, it takes decades of work to add a missing variable or a new alphabet to the equation that is closer to reality than the original one.

Dr. Parker opened the newly arrived WhatsApp message from an unknown number. Drops of sweat started rolling behind his ears when he saw his son Rachit tied to a chair with his mouth sealed. Every significant moment of Rachit's life in the last 15 years passed in 15 seconds before his eyes. A storm of thoughts started in his mind about what he would say to his wife. After all, Rachit was the epicentre of their life. Their only child.

Suddenly, the ringtone, which was a black hole sound captured by NASA, broke the chain of Dr. Parker's thoughts. Dr. Parker picked up the call from the same unknown number.

"I hope you are convinced about your son's kidnapping," said the man on the other side.

"What do you want?" said Dr. Parker while gulping saliva.

"You will soon find out, Dr. Parker." There is a car waiting for you outside. Get inside as soon as possible. You know what is at stake.

Dr. Parker got outside and saw a black car.

"PU—1403—an interesting number for a car. 14th March is Albert Einstein's birthday. Is the car owner Einstein's fan or what?" Dr. Parker asked the car driver, who had a mask on his face.

"I am not supposed to talk, sir," said the driver. "Anyways, shall we go?"

"Of course, do I have an option?" Dr. Parker replied.

After 2 hours of travel, Dr. Parker found himself in a dark jungle. There were large trees of Deodar and little shrubs all around him. The only sound that reached his ears was those chirping crickets. The moon was the only natural light source in the jungle, apart from those glow-worms trying to win the mating game.

Dr. Parker looked around to find himself all alone. The driver had left too. Dr. Parker did see some pairs of glowing eyes of the typical jungle predators. However, this was not the right kind of company he wanted.

"Welcome, Dr. Parker."

A voice from an unknown source hit Dr. Parker's ear drums.

"The wait is finally over. We have 'the Dr. Pragyan Parker with us'. By the way, hearty congratulations for being recognised as the most influential scientist and educator in the world. I believe we have got the right person for the job," said the kidnapper.

"Thank you so much for your kind wishes. I am still confused about why someone would kidnap my son. I am neither a billionaire nor a politician. So you would get nothing out of me. I don't think I have anything that could lure you into kidnapping my son," replied Dr. Parker.

Kidnapper: "Not everybody in this universe needs money. Now let us understand the rules of the game."

Dr. Parker: "Game, what game?"

Kidnapper: "I will ask you some questions. Based on the quality of the answers, you will be provided with a clue about how to trace Rachit.

"You must answer our questions in a way that engages our listeners. High school students in this jungle will be listening to your answers. Of course, they will not be visible to you. After every answer, we will take their polls and inform you if you successfully engaged our students. You will get details on reaching Rachit with every correct and engaging answer.

"By the way, we have already poisoned your son. We fulfilled his wish for a pizza but with toppings of poisonous mushrooms. You have 3 hours. That's it. The poison must have started to work by now. The clock is ticking, Dr. Parker, and for you, every microsecond counts.

"Give correct and engaging answers and take Rachit back with you. Give wrong and boring answers and take Rachit back with you. In the second scenario, you would take a dead Rachit. I hope I am clear."

Dr. Parker's mouth went dry. His heart started racing as adrenaline tried to control his body. He knew what was at stake. He was a patriot, and he wanted his research on teaching methodology to benefit his motherland.

Dr. Parker was reluctant to share his research secrets with a kidnapper who might be from a different country or a planet altogether. Motherland and son were both close to his heart. However, this time, he had to choose between the two.

Kidnapper: "Before you teach us your secret learning technique, we would like to test you on some fundamental aspects of science. So we will ask questions about a chapter often perceived as boring by a large number of students preparing for the 12th standard. The name of the chapter is 'Chemistry in Daily Life,' which was part of the older version of the textbooks. Students had to memorise difficult names, and those inclined toward maths often found it irrelevant. Your job is to turn a highly boring chapter into something that our students would go crazy about. So, the quality of your answers would decide if you would take Rachit back home and celebrate or mourn his dead body. And yes, this is the right time to show off your sense of humour. So give your best, Dr. Parker."

Dr. Parker: "Before I start discussing the chapter on chemistry in daily life, I would like to discuss something relevant to this place."

Kidnapper: "You mean this forest?"

Dr. Parker: "Yes, I mean this forest."

Kidnapper: "If it is interesting, I would love for you to proceed. Please go ahead."

Dr. Parker: "Do you know that these trees in this giant forest are talking to each other now?"

Kidnapper: "What did you eat for breakfast, Dr. Parker? Are you out of your mind? You have been called here to discuss science and not some superstitious nonsense."

Dr. Parker: "I am a scientist. And I can only make bold claims with solid evidence backing them. So allow me to continue. I am well aware that an extraordinary claim requires extraordinary evidence."

Kidnapper: "I hope you realise that your son's life is at stake."

Dr. Parker: "Of course, Mr. Kidnapper. I do realise that."

Kidnapper: "Go on in that case. Continue your forest story."

Dr. Parker: "Have you heard of Suzanne Simard?"

Kidnapper: "Not really."

Dr. Parker: "She is a Canadian scientist known for her research on communication among forest trees. Simard, using modern science tools, has listened to these talking trees for the first time.

"Dr. Simard has shown that trees communicate with each other via a network of fungi spread across their root systems.

"The 'Mycorrhizae' fungi are the postmen of the forest communication network. The fungi and the trees mutually agree to help each other, a relationship that we call symbiosis in biology.

"The fungus does not make its food and is, hence, dependent on the trees for its bread and butter. The trees use the fungal network to send nutrients, and danger signals to other trees.

"One of the most exciting discoveries of Simard's research is the 'Mother trees.'"

Kidnapper: "Mother trees?"

Dr. Parker: "Yup, the mother trees."

"As per what we know so far, and this is still a hypothesis, Mother trees, the largest and oldest in the forest network, are known to nurture their seedlings and relatives. They do this by directing a substantial portion of nutrients and resources towards them.

"Apart from being a good mother, the trees are also known to help struggling neighbours. In times of emergency and stress, the mother trees increase the flow of nutrients towards them to aid their survival."

Kidnapper: "This is so goddamn interesting. Tell me more."

Dr. Parker: "Trees communicate not only through fungal networks but also via hormones and slow-pulsing electrical signals.

"What we have learned so far could be the tip of the iceberg.

"There's likely a complex social network within forests, operating and undergoing unnoticed under our noses. The insights from evolutionary biology could help us understand these communications. However, we need more evidence to show that this communication is intentional.

"A group of scientists also believe that the concept of mother trees is far-fetched. They think that transferring nutrients from one tree to another could be unintentional. A regular releasing and picking up of stuff moving around without any intentional transfer. I guess we need to conduct more research before making 'Mother trees' part of our textbooks. Even Einstein's general relativity is made to pass through tests now and then, and so must any other idea that promises a radical change in how we see our world. Healthy skepticism is the foundation of science. However, whatever we have learned is possibly one of the most exciting scientific research studies in recent times."

Kidnapper: "I agree. Everything that you have shared is fascinating."

Dr. Parker: "In that case, let me intrigue you more.

"Significant communication among trees happens via chemical messengers called Volatile organic compounds (VOCs). One of the most exciting examples of using VOCs for communication comes from the acacia tree. Let me share a story about Giraffes.

"Giraffes are herbivores with a heart that weighs about 11 kg. Their blood pressure is double that of humans."

Kidnapper: "Interesting, for sure. It makes logical sense for giraffes to have strong hearts as they have to pump so much blood against gravity. An intense pressure would be required to supply blood to the brain hanging at such a height."

Dr. Parker: "You are right. The heart has to be strong enough to pump blood to the giraffe's brain. I often wonder about the hearts of those gigantic dinosaurs."

Kidnapper: "Oh yes. That's a question worth pondering. Anyways, let us continue with your giraffe story."

Dr. Parker: "Yes. These giraffes love to eat the leaves of acacia trees. The depth of this love could be guessed from the fact that giraffes eat up to 26 kg of acacia daily."

Kidnapper: "26 kg leaves in a day! How would the tree survive in such a case? Doesn't this over-munching affect the survival of the acacia too?"

Dr. Parker: "Irrespective of whether you succeed in life in materialistic terms, biologically life has no meaning if you fail to send your genes to the next generation. Survival and reproduction are the only biological goals that nature cares for. The rest of all is your self-invented struggle created to satisfy the ego.

"You are right. The giraffe does challenge the survival of acacia. However, trees have invented strategies to deal with these giant herbivores. Acacia here does something super interesting."

Kidnapper: "I would love to know about the defence mechanism of acacia you are talking about."

Dr. Parker: "Acacia has long-pointed thorns. These thorns are strong and pointed enough to poke holes easily

into the tongue of an animal trying to eat acacia leaves. This is the first line of defence used by acacia."

Kidnapper: "Wow. This sounds similar to the fences you see at the international borders."

Dr. Parker: "Yes. You could say that."

Kidnapper: "But I am sure that the giraffes have found a way to protect themselves from those pointed thorns; otherwise, why would they successfully eat such a quantity of acacia leaves in a day?"

Dr. Parker: "Exactly. The giraffes have developed flexible tongues that can whirl around those sharp thorns and pluck the leaves."

Kidnapper: "Holy shit. That sounds super fun. Wow."

Dr. Parker: "The acacia does something else to beat the giraffes in this survival race.

"Acacias can sense if the giraffes are eating their leaves. Once detected, they can immediately pump chemicals called 'tannins' into their leaves."

Kidnapper: "How would tannins help here?"

Dr. Parker: "The tannins spoil the giraffe's party. Tannins are bitter and also mess up the giraffe's digestive system. Both of these effects slow down the giraffe's ability to eat leaves. The tannins are toxic in higher concentrations and could also kill animals like kudus."

Kidnapper: "Eating the leaves rich with tannins is like eating a bitter gourd wrapped up with a thick film of chocolate."

Dr. Parker: "Exactly. However, the acacia don't stop at this.

"Acacia has developed further defence mechanisms against greedy giraffe's uncontrolled munching of leaves."

Kidnapper: "Like what?"

Dr. Parker: "The acacia trees release ethylene gas."

Kidnapper: "Ethylene gas?"

Dr. Parker: "The ethylene gas released by one acacia tree is detected by the neighbouring acacia trees, so they, too, start producing tannins before the giraffes come to them. It is like a mutual agreement among the acacia trees, where they inform each other about the upcoming danger from the giraffes via the release of chemicals in the air."

Kidnapper: "This is what you implied by the trees talking to each other. The acacia whose leaves are being eaten informs the other trees through a chemical signal.

The neighbouring acacia detects the signal and responds by pumping tannin into the leaves beforehand. This makes the leaves bitter even before the giraffes start munching. This is so amazing. It is absolutely mind-boggling.

"So the acacia trees finally defeated the giraffes?"

Dr. Parker: "Not really. There is a slight twist in the story."

Kidnapper: "Listening. Go on."

Dr. Parker: "The giraffes haven't given up yet. They have figured out that the ethylene signal cannot travel more than 50 yards. Therefore, they start with the next acacia tree, much more than 50 yards away from the first acacia tree. Brilliant? Isn't it?"

Kidnapper: "How does the giraffe know that acacia's signal would not travel farther than 50 yards? Did he read somewhere, too?"

Dr. Parker: "Giraffes could have learned this from experience."

Kidnapper: "Man, this is out of this world. I never knew that biology was so interesting. I wish our schools started teaching biology with examples like this."

Dr. Parker: "I wanted to share something more about this giraffe story."

Kidnapper: "Sure. I would love to hear and so do my students."

Dr. Parker: "The acacia has another layer of defence to protect its precious leaves from being eaten by the giraffe.

"Bull-Horn acacia in South and Central America rely on ants instead of tannins to deter the herbivores. Natural selection has modified the thorns of bull-horn acacia to provide the ants with a sweet home. Along with the shelter the acacia also helps the ants with food. These ants get energy from the sugar present in the nectar which is produced near the tip of the thorns. Recent research has also shown that the acacia makes ants dependent on its nectar. The ants are not able to digest sugar from any other sources except the acacia nectar laden with the required digestive enzyme.

"Acacia blocks the development of sugar-digesting enzyme among the ants with the enzyme blockers present in the nectar. This strategy makes the ant dependent and addicted to acacia's sugary nectar. The innocent ants return this so-called favour by guarding acacia against the herbivores that munch on the leaves of their landlords.

"What I find extremely interesting is that the acacia manage to call the army of ants as soon as they find herbivores eating up their leaves. Researchers from Cornell University have shown that the concentration of ants near the damaged site increases by 400% within minutes of the damage caused by the herbivores. Irrespective of its size, a friend in need is a friend indeed."

Kidnapper: "So cool."

Dr. Parker: "The story about the giraffe is just the tip of the iceberg, as there is so much more that plants do. Recently, there has been a sudden surge among plant biologists worldwide eager to explore the concept of intelligence in plants. This idea, which had been lying dormant for a long time, is now ripe for deeper exploration as mainstream science takes a genuine interest in it. I would like to discuss some other intriguing examples of plant communication."

Kidnapper: "The story about the giraffe was extraordinary. We are eager to learn what else is in your Pandora's box. However, before we start discussing a new topic I would like you to answer questions from my students."

Dr. Parker: "I love students who ask questions. Every major scientific discovery could be linked to someone asking a profound question".

Kidnapper: "I agree. One of my students is curious about how giraffes manage to protect themselves from the effects of such high blood pressure. For humans, persistent high blood pressure is known to cause kidney damage, damage to the tissues in the heart, swelling and risk of dying from strokes. However the giraffe is found to be immune to all these medical problems. What exact solutions has natural selection gifted giraffes to protect them naturally from the side-effects of the chronic high blood pressure."

Dr. Parker: "Wow. Questions of such level could only come from students who are deeply passionate about understanding a topic. We do have some answers for these questions on giraffe's cardiovascular system. However it is still an ongoing area of research and I am sure there is so much we are going to uncover in the future.

"Barbara Natterson Horowitz, a scientist affiliated with Harvard University and UCLA has shed some light on this from the lens of evolutionary biology. They found that in spite of such high blood pressure and thickening of the walls of ventricles, the heart tissues do not get damaged. In short you do not find any fibrosis among the heart tissues of the giraffe. Fibrosis is a condition where excessive wear and tear due to persistent high blood pressure causes tissue damage. This leads to scars and deposition of collagen which decreases the overall pumping capacity of the heart.

"The giraffe also has a unique cardiac rhythm that delicately balances the volume of blood across the different chambers of the giraffe's heart. This allows the heart to pump more blood with each stroke, allowing a giraffe to run hard despite its thicker heart muscle. The giraffes also carry some 5 different genes linked to fibrosis."

Kidnapper: "This was a brilliant answer Dr. Parker.

"Studying the similar anatomical and physiological processes of different animals can teach us a great deal about our own biology and diseases."

Dr. Parker: "The giraffe story was all about how one plant can alert another during an attack. However, in some cases, plants emit signals to attract insect assassins to eliminate the insects eating their leaves."

Kidnapper: "Insect assassins? That sounds cool."

Dr. Parker: "Yes, for example, when tomato plants realise a caterpillar is eating their leaves, they emit a chemical that alerts the caterpillar assassins around them. A parasitoid wasp picks up this signal—the insect assassin in this case. Guided by the signal, the wasp locates the caterpillar and lays an egg inside it. As the larva grows, it consumes the caterpillar, ultimately causing its death."

Kidnapper: "That's an intriguing method of self-protection. However, I have a question from one of our students. It is this, 'Could the caterpillar retaliate and silence the tomato plant, or somehow interfere with their chemical communication with the wasps? As in the case of the acacia and giraffe, could the caterpillar find a way to stop the tomato from releasing those signals and attract the killer wasp?'"

Dr. Parker: "That's an excellent question. Recent research has shown that caterpillars try to prevent the tomato plant from getting in touch with the parasitoid wasps. The enzymes in the saliva of the caterpillar help mediate this effect. The leaves of the plants have tiny pores called stomata. Stomata control the release of gases and defence chemicals. A team of researchers found that tomato hornworm caterpillars induce the closure of the stomata in the host plant within 5 minutes of them eating the leaves. The stomata remain closed for almost 48 hours, preventing the tomato plant from seeking help from the wasps. Scientists have also found similar effects on other plants."

Kidnapper: "Let me sprinkle some water on my eyes. I am not sure if I am dreaming or fully awake. What you said is so fantastic to be true."

Dr. Parker: "What amazes me is that different wasps attack different caterpillars, and the plant can summon all of them at various times through a unique chemical. It's as if each has a unique phone number that the plant dials to invite them for the attack."

Kidnapper: "But my question is this: How does the plant identify which leaf eater is causing the damage? Without identifying the correct herbivores, attracting the right assassin or the insect killer wouldn't be possible. How does the plant differentiate among the various insects feasting on their leaves?"

Dr. Parker: "I can see where you're coming from. Plants can taste and detect the chemicals present in the saliva of each caterpillar species and other herbivores. The compounds in the insect's saliva serve as a 'unique ID' that plants use to recognise unwelcome guests. Once the herbivore is identified, the plant releases specific volatile organic chemicals targeting the relevant parasitoid wasp. Scientists in Japan caught the plants talking to each other via the release of chemicals in real-time. The Japanese scientists modified these plants to glow once they detected a chemical message from another plant. This experiment was brilliant in capturing what was hidden from our eyes."

Kidnapper: "I never thought plants could demonstrate such a sophisticated level of communication mechanisms. Is there more to their intelligence?"

Dr. Parker: "There is more, of course. I will move on to more sophisticated signs of intelligence among plants later, but first, I'd like to talk about *Rafflesia*."

Kidnapper: "*Rafflesia*? You mean those gigantic flowers."

Dr. Parker: "Yes, there's much more to *Rafflesia* than its size. The transfer of pollens from one flower to another is one of the most important aspects of reproduction among flowering plants. Since plants cannot move and deliberately put their pollen into another flower, they take the help of water and wind as well as animals like honey bees, beetles, wasps, flies, butterflies, moths, humming birds, and even bats to transport their pollen. We call these courier guys for plants as pollinating agents. But why would these animal pollinating agents bother themselves to transport the pollen of plants? The answer is that these innocent pollinating agents never realise that they are unknowingly helping the plants with one of the most important biological unions. The plants, on the other hand, offer every possible incentive to attract the pollinating agents. The beautiful, bright, colourful patterns we humans have admired about the flowers are to attract the pollinators, not us. Nectar is another thing that lures the pollinators to enter the flower. The nectar is rich in sugars and fulfills the energy requirement of the pollinators. The pollens are also in the lunch menu of the bees and certain wasps. The bees use pollens to feed their broods back home as they are rich in proteins, lipids and antioxidants.

"You see luring the pollinating agents isn't restricted to offering nectar and pollen as well as those attractive and colourful floral patterns. The flowers also appeal to other senses of the pollinating agents as well. For example, the plants produce a pleasant smell to attract the pollinating moths that roam at night.

"The pollinating agents have to brush up against the stamen during their quest to feed on the nectar. Meanwhile the sticky pollen grains from the stamen cling to the pollinating agents and accompany them to the next flower. In short the pollinating agents help the plants with their ultimate evolutionary duty.

"Now coming to *Rafflesia*. Natural selection has equipped *Rafflesia* with one of the most fascinating pollination strategies. To transfer its pollen, *Rafflesia* is at the mercy of carrion flies. However, unlike other flowers, *Rafflesia* has nothing to offer in return."

Kidnapper: "Then why would a carrion fly visit *Rafflesia*?"

Dr. Parker: "Carrion flies are attracted to rotting meat or decaying flesh. I know it sounds unpleasant, but our perception of the world is highly subjective. What attracts one species may repel another. In that rotting meat, carrion flies find the perfect spot to lay their eggs.

"*Rafflesia* blooms for only a short period, and during this time, it increases its temperature."

Kidnapper: "Why would it do that?"

Dr. Parker: "To attract the carrion flies, *Rafflesia* produces a smell similar to rotting meat. If you observe its colour, you'll notice a striking resemblance to what rotting meat looks like. The molecules that smell like decaying flesh produced by the flower must travel far and wide so that the carrion flies could detect them."

Kidnapper: "Okay, I understand. The flower heats up to help evaporate the smelly molecules, allowing them to travel farther and enhance the probability of being picked up by the carrion flies."

Dr. Parker: "Exactly. Researchers who have analysed the molecules produced by *Rafflesia* found them to match those coming out of rotting meat. In short, the *Rafflesia* tries its best to smell and look like rotting meat to fool the carrion flies. It's an incredible example of molecular mimicry.

"Another interesting aspect of *Rafflesia*'s pollination strategy involves its pollen. Unlike most of the pollens that are powdery, *Rafflesia*'s pollen is a thick liquid that sticks to the carrion fly's body. It remains there for days. This sticky and durable pollen is a masterstroke since the fly might travel up to 12 to 15 miles before finding another *Rafflesia*. The stickiness and durability of the pollen ensures that it survives the long journey and successfully fertilises another *Rafflesia*."

Kidnapper: "It's remarkable how natural selection can engineer such perfect adaptations for species dependent on each other. Famous evolutionary biologist Richard Dawkins rightly said that nature is a blind watchmaker. The analogy celebrates the randomness of natural selection in creating adaptations that seem intentionally perfect. However, these adaptations that seem perfectly designed from the outside have evolved over a very large timescale. The adaptations are certainly not intentional. Natural selection, despite its creativity and skill, remains blind."

Dr. Parker: "So well said."

Kidnapper: "Are there any other flowers that use similar strategy to fool their pollinating agents? I mean there has to be some other flowers too who would have faced similar challenges as *Rafflesia*".

Dr. Parker: "Yes. There are couple of them like the Vodoolily and the flowers from the genus *Arum*.

"There are many flowers from the *Arum* genus that produce foul smelling molecules to lure bees and flies that love to roam around dung and urine. Some of these species also produce the smell of rotting flesh like *Rafflesia*. However the strategy among the *Arum* flowers is more intriguing. The *Arum* flower does something extraordinary to ensure its pollen reaches the right target."

Kidnapper: "What could be even more bizarre than what *Rafflesia* does to attract the carrion flies?"

Dr. Parker: "The *Arum* flowers keep the flies hostage for 24 hours or sometimes upto two days. The flies are trapped and kept inside till they are bathed in pollen or done with fertilisation if they were already carrying pollen with them. Once the job is done the captive flies are released."

Kidnapper: "Really? The flower actually does not let the fly go for almost 24 hours?"

Dr. Parker: "Nature has its own style of doing things."

Kidnapper: "That was so interesting Dr. Parker."

Dr. Parker: "Now, let me introduce you to another bizarre plant communication and intelligence mystery yet to be solved. Have you ever heard of vines?"

Kidnapper: "Yes, vines are plants with poor support systems that climb on host plants using tendrils. But what's so mysterious about vines?"

Dr. Parker: "Ernesto Gianoli, a plant ecologist in Chile, stumbled upon a magical discovery during a walk in a Chilean rainforest. He observed a vine doing something that has made plant experts worldwide scratch their heads.

"Dr. Gianoli was observing a shrub called 'arrayan.' While observing the leaves of the shrub, he noticed that similar leaves were also attached to a different, thinner stem that whirled around the shrub. After closely observing, he found that those leaves belonged to a vine, *Boquila trifoliolata*. He was aware of how the *Boquila trifoliolata* leaves looked. He immediately realized that the vine was doing its best to copy 'arrayan.' It was trying to hide by camouflaging with the host shrub - an interesting strategy that plants use to prevent herbivores from eating their leaves. But there was something more to this mimicry. The next thing I am going to share is one of the most bizarre powers ever gifted to a plant by natural selection."

Kidnapper: "Why would you say that? Isn't mimicry normal in biology?"

Dr. Parker: "Dr. Gianoli discovered that the vine was imitating the colour, shape, size, orientation, petiole length, and other features of the leaves of the host plant it climbs. This, however, is not the most surprising part. He found that the vine can copy the leaf features of about 20 different plant species. But even this is not the most astonishing aspect of this vine."

Kidnapper: "What did you just say? A single plant can mimic the leaf features of around 20 different plants, and you're saying that's still not the most surprising feature? What else can the plant do - play YouTube videos?"

Dr. Parker: "Not really. The plant can copy the leaves of different plants simultaneously if it climbs two of them."

Kidnapper: "Man, this is bizarre. Do we have any clue how the plant manages this? What's the exact mechanism? How does it know which features to copy and so precisely?"

Dr. Parker: "The most intriguing part of this plant is yet to come. In 2021, a researcher and citizen scientist published a paper with everyone talking. They placed the vine next to an artificial plastic plant, and the vine mimicked the features of the artificial plant too. Unlike some plants, this vine can mimic those around it without physical contact.

"The researchers suggest that these vines somehow 'see' the plants around them and mimic their exact patterns. They speculate an undiscovered mechanism that enables plants to observe and take note of their surroundings. The researchers have gone far to suggest that the vines might have cells that work like a lens in the human eye, capturing visual data. Although this paper has faced significant criticism for its experiment design and data interpretation, scientists are open to exploring these possibilities, no matter how bizarre. It's just that they are not yet satisfied with the findings of this particular paper. Researchers strongly believe this vine presents an incredible opportunity to uncover fundamental aspects of plant biology.

"I strongly believe in not dismissing an idea outright, as the history of science is full of instances where ideas once deemed impossible or weird later gained acceptance. Some of the greatest scientific breakthroughs, like Darwin's evolution by natural selection, heliocentrism, continental Drift, the Big Bang, and most importantly, "quantum mechanics," were initially ridiculed. Let me cite Max Planck here,

*"A new scientific truth does not triumph by convincing its opponents and making them see the light, but rather because its opponents eventually die, and a new generation grows up familiar with it."*

Kidnapper: "I agree with you there. Ideas that challenge established theories often face the strongest resistance. But we must focus on evidence and judge accordingly. Apart from the idea that these chameleon vines can see other plants and copy their features, is there an alternate hypothesis to explain their mimicry mechanism?"

Dr. Parker: "Yes, there is. Dr. Gianoli proposed two alternative hypothesis to explain the vine's remarkable mimicry ability. One theory suggests that the plants detect volatile organic compounds released by the host plant to execute this enigmatic feat. The other hypothesis is that the plants engage in horizontal gene transfer to exchange information."

Kidnapper: "This is interesting. However, our students have a question?"

Dr. Parker: "Sure. I would love to answer them."

Kidnapper: "Can you comment on plant consciousness and intelligence?"

Dr. Parker: "The topic of plant intelligence and consciousness is somewhat controversial. It is also important to approach this cautiously. We often judge intelligence from a human-centric perspective, expecting every intelligent species to have a complex nervous system like ours. It should be noted that different species face unique environmental challenges and don't necessarily need to solve problems like we do. Intelligence should be considered a collection of qualities like learning, problem-solving, communication, memory, self-awareness, social complexity, and other behaviours. While we don't know of any plant that exhibits all these traits, the examples shared so far suggest that plants possess many traits indicative of intelligence. Let me share some more examples.

"Research has shown that the root tips of plants and trees can know if a neighbouring plant is a relative or belongs to a different species."

Kidnapper: "You mean that plants can sense if they are growing next to their brothers and sisters or a stranger."

Dr. Parker: "Yes.

"We also have evidence that plants like 'touch-me-not' or *Mimosa pudica* can remember certain movements for up to a long time.

"Do you know why those 'Touch-me-not' or *Mimosa pudica* plants are so sensitive to touch and close their leaves? There has to be a reason for such specific behaviour."

Kidnapper: "It is an interesting question, for sure. For the plants, the biggest survival threat comes from the herbivores. I am guessing the closing of leaves in the case of *Mimosa* would have evolved as a defence mechanism against those herbivores."

Dr. Parker: "Exactly. *Mimosa* close their leaves to fool and surprise the leaf-eating animals. Many of these herbivores might change their minds after seeing this leaf-closing response from *Mimosa*. It might surprise and frighten them to think that the *Mimosa* is not the right lunch item for them."

Kidnapper: "Wow. I never knew that *Mimosa's* ability to close the leaves had such deep evolutionary reasons."

Dr. Parker: "*Mimosa* have also evolved an ability to differentiate whether a movement is a real threat from herbivores or harmless. It would not make sense to close your leaves for a stimulus that comes frequently but is harmless.

"Let's say you are taking *Mimosa* plants to your village, and you come across 20 different bumpers along the journey. The plant might close its leaves initially but may not respond after the 10th bump. It is as if the plant learns that the movement related to the bumper is harmless. The sensitivity towards the harmless movement or stimulus will drop, and the plant might keep this in its memory for a long time. The plant may not respond to bumper-type movements for some 40 days. The plant will normally respond to other stimuli, though.

"There's a growing interest in understanding plant behaviour, particularly regarding intelligence. With all the expensive science toys we have today, nothing stops us from making further discoveries. If Indian scientist Jagadish Chandra Bose could conduct pioneering studies on plant intelligence in 1926, then with all the modern tools at our disposal, we can certainly advance this field now."

Kidnapper: "I thought J.C. Bose was known as the father of wireless communication. He was also the first to produce microwaves and did pioneering work in semiconductors. I never knew he studied plant intelligence."

Dr. Parker: "J.C. Bose was a pioneer in studying plant intelligence and communication. He invented instruments like the crescograph to measure minute growths in plants and studied their electrical potential, proposing the idea that plants have a developed nervous system. His work on plant intelligence and other aspects is detailed in his 1926 book 'The Nervous Mechanisms of Plants.' Bose argued that electrical signals control the movement of leaves in the 'touch-me-not' or the *Mimosa* plant. Dr. Bose was far ahead of his time, and plant biologists worldwide are now recognising his contributions to plant communication and intelligence. Although his ideas about electrical impulses in plants initially faced massive opposition, he received support from renowned scientists like Lord Kelvin, Rayleigh, and J.J. Thomson during his England visit. It was Rayleigh who assisted Bose in getting his papers published. Bose also delivered the famous Friday evening lectures initiated by Michael Faraday. There is something more to J.C. Bose that makes him stand out as a scientist."

Kidnapper: "Like what?"

Dr. Parker: "Jagadish Chandra Bose believed in the free dissemination of knowledge and was strictly against patenting his inventions.

"Let me ask you a question."

Kidnapper: "Sure."

Dr. Parker: "Have you heard of cosmic microwave background radiation?"

Kidnapper: "Yes, I do. Cosmic microwave background radiation is the oldest light in the universe, formed 380,000 years after the Big Bang. According to our current understanding, the Big Bang led to the birth of our universe and everything else we know. The latest data indicates that this rapid expansion (not explosion as commonly believed) of space happened 13.77 billion years ago. Initially, the temperature was so hot that it prevented the marriage of electrons and protons for a long time. The pious union of these subatomic particles happened only when the universe cooled enough for these particles to combine and form an atom. The first atom was thus formed some 380,000 years ago, producing the oldest light in the universe, making the universe transparent to light.

"The original radiation belonged to the visible and infrared spectrum. However, as the universe expanded and space stretched, so did the wavelength of this light, turning it into low-energy microwaves. Cosmic microwave background radiation was bound to permeate the fabric of spacetime if the Big Bang were true. Therefore, the discovery of this fossil radiation provided the strongest evidence in favour of the Big Bang hypothesis. The microwave whisper also turned out to be the last nail in the coffin for competing scientific models of the time. Measuring and studying the cosmic microwave background radiation is all about understanding the early days of our universe. Can there be a quest more profound than understanding the origin of what exists today and what existed before us?"

Dr. Parker: "Wow. I am impressed by your knowledge. Why would you become a kidnapper?"

Kidnapper: "None of your business, Dr. Parker."

Dr. Parker: "I have another question in that case."

Kidnapper: "We discussed Dr. J.C. Bose and his contributions to plant intelligence. Why are we talking about cosmology here?"

Dr. Parker: "Please answer my question. You must be aware that radio astronomers Arno Penzias and Robert Wilson discovered the cosmic microwave background radiation in 1965."

Kidnapper: "Of course, I am aware. Penzias and Wilson initially thought that their Nobel-prize-winning noise was coming from the pigeon shit lying on the antenna. However, the noise continued even when they got the setup free of pigeons. It came from every direction."

Dr. Parker: "Awesome. What setup do they use?"

Kidnapper: "They used a **'Holmdel Horn Antenna,'** which was a large microwave horn antenna."

Dr. Parker: "Can you tell me who invented the first 'horn antenna'?"

Kidnapper: "Sorry, I have no clue about this."

Dr. Parker: "While doing his pioneering experiments with microwaves, Jagdish Chandra Bose invented the world's first horn antenna. Yet Dr. J.C Bose did not patent most of his inventions that had such an enormous impact on the world."

Kidnapper: "I am impressed with the things shared so far. However, it is the students who would decide

*The Holmdel Horn Antenna, with which Penzias and Wilson discovered the cosmic microwave background radiation.*

*Indian physicist J.C. Bose (seen here) at the University of Calcutta flared out the end of a waveguide, demonstrating the horn antenna.*

Rachit's fate. Check your WhatsApp for the poll result. If things are positive, you will get clues on how to reach Rachit."

Dr. Parker received a notification on his WhatsApp: "Congratulations, Dr. Parker. 85% of the students liked what you shared. Move by 2000 steps in the north, and you will be a bit closer to Rachit." Dr. Parker looked up and thanked God for this tiny victory. Dr. Parker walked some 2000 steps and waited for the next instructions. He knew he was running out of time. However, he also had to do his best to save Rachit. He knew what lay ahead was not easy.

Kidnapper: "Congratulations, Dr. Parker. You have moved closer to your goal. Let us now jump straight away to Chemistry in Daily life. Most students have often perceived this chapter to be boring."

Dr. Parker: "I agree entirely with you on this."

Kidnapper: "Here comes my first question. Please tell us who Paul Ehrlich was."

Dr. Parker: "Paul Ehrlich was a 19th-century German Scientist. He is considered to be the father of chemotherapy."

Kidnapper: "Is the word chemotherapy used in the textbook the same chemotherapy term used in the context of cancer?"

Dr. Parker: "Chemotherapy is all about using chemicals to treat diseases. Although people associate the term solely with cancer these days.

"The idea that chemicals could be used to cure diseases is one of the most critical ideas that humanity has ever conceived. Interestingly, the growth of the dye industry catalysed the birth of chemotherapy. It all started with the first synthetic dye.

"You would be amazed to know that 18-year-old William Perkin discovered a dye that sowed the seeds of the modern dye industry in his private laboratory. As the dye industry flourished in Germany, it contributed directly to the birth of chemotherapy."

Kidnapper: "Can you go deeper into the details of this discovery?"

Dr. Parker: "Sure. William Perkin was born in England. For a time, Perkin thought of becoming an artist, as he had a great interest in painting. However, he fell in love with chemistry after he saw his friend performing some experiments with crystals before his thirteenth birthday.

"In Perkin's time, chemistry was still in its infancy, and little was taught in the country. He was lucky to get admission to a school in London that offered chemistry lessons. Thomas Hall, the chemistry instructor, taught twice a week during the lunch hours. Thomas realised Perkin's love for chemistry, which made him assist in the lecture experiments. Perkin enjoyed working in the school laboratory. On the other hand, Perkin's father wanted him to pursue Architecture as he saw no financial security in chemistry.

"This was an era ahead of billion-dollar chemical industries and university departments that would have a massive impact on the world. People in those days had no idea that chemistry research would reap some of the most valuable benefits for mankind. Everything was going to be a gift from chemistry, from painkillers to paints. Most people who could fund the opening of a chemistry department saw nothing of practical value in the subject. Justus Von Liebig from Germany seeded the idea of promoting chemistry among the rich and royals of England. Taken by the lure of getting something for commercial use, the people of influence established the Royal College of Chemistry in London. Liebig's student, August Hofmann, was appointed as the college's first director.

"August Hofmann was a passionate researcher and teacher who brought Liebig's tradition of experimental organic chemistry to London. Hofmann's teaching style enchanted his students, as he could pass on the baton of awe to them. He knew which projects to assign and took a deep interest in their work as if each were extremely important. During one of his regular chemistry experiments, he asked a student to pour sulphuric acid into a test-tube. The acid fell, with some drops entering Hofmann's eyes. He was made to rest in a dark room for weeks to recover at the earliest. But even during this tragedy, Hofmann interacted with his students to keep track of their work and impart instructions."

Kidnapper: "That speaks volumes about his integrity and dedication as a teacher."

Dr. Parker: "It does. During 5 years under Hofmann, some 36 projects were undertaken. However, none of these created anything valuable for the patrons of the institute. Since the institute failed to deliver what it promised, the fund donors decided to pull the plug, and the Royal College of Chemistry was made to merge with the School of Mines. On the other side, Hofmann was unwilling to give up and thought that his experiments could give England one of the most sought-after molecules. Can you guess the name of this molecule that the Britishers wanted so badly?"

Kidnapper: "It could be a painkiller. And if not painkiller then it must be those colourful dye. The rapidly growing textile industry in England badly wanted them."

Dr. Parker: "None of that. England desperately wanted a way to manufacture Quinine those days. Malaria was one of the most significant barriers that hindered Britishers from rapidly expanding their colonies. This was a time when the cause and vector of malaria were unknown. The disease was widespread in Asia and Africa and a menace in France, Holland, and Italy. Quinine - the only known cure - was sold at an exorbitant price. The East India Company spent approximately £100,000 annually on Quinine. The natural supply was limited, so making it in the lab could have been the most desirable result that the British Royals wanted.

"Hofmann believed in the magic of chemistry and its potential to create new natural products like Quinine by playing with molecules of similar formulas. He shared this idea with his star student, Perkin, who had the skills to make new chemicals.

"Perkin had a private laboratory at home. This was not a state-of-the-art lab setup but more of an amateur basic collection of chemical bottles, test tubes, and furnaces. What's important is that he just had the right chemical ingredients to create a compound that would change the world. As Hoffmann told Perkin, the recipe to make Quinine was simple. Take a base that resembles Quinine in its formula and add some water. Naphthalene was the most apt base in this case. Perkin mixed the base with water and found a reddish compound instead of Quinine. He repeated his experiment with Aniline and was surprised to see a black-coloured compound this time. He purified and dried the compound. Making the material react with alcohol gave the Mauve dye. Because of his outstanding experimental skills, Perkin could isolate 5 per cent of the material responsible for the colour.

"Perkin decided to test his newly discovered dye on silk. This was a lustrous and brilliant colour that did not fade with washing, nor was it affected by prolonged exposure to light. Perkin had yet to learn about the true potential of his discovery, and hence, he sought guidance from his friend. He sent a sample of fabric to a dye work owner in Scotland.

"Robert Pullar, the young owner, replied enthusiastically, saying that it was one of the most valuable things developed recently. He saw that Perkin's dye had clear superiority over existing dyes and would be revolutionary if cheap. The purple texture was also the most sought-after among the ultra-rich and royals. In short, Perkin was sitting on a gold mine.

"Perkin and his friend were only willing to share their discovery with Hofmann if they did more experiments. However, Hofmann, after being made aware of the discovery, wasn't quite happy. He saw dyes as a byproduct of regular chemistry accidents. He thought it was foolish of Perkin to give up his research career to commercialize his newly discovered dye.

"Perkin, with the help of his relatives and friends, set up a factory to manufacture Mauve dye. Mauve was a massive hit among people as it made their lives colourful. The discovery also altered the perception that chemistry was merely a theoretical branch with no industrial applications."

Kidnapper: "Indeed. From what you have shared so far, Perkin's accidental discovery of Mauve changed how people treated chemistry and chemists. But we are still waiting for the life-saving medicines to enter the picture."

Dr. Parker: "Perkin's discovery of Aniline Mauve could be considered one of the most important events in mankind's history. The discovery of this first synthetic dye led to a massive boom in dye manufacturing. However, the country where dye and other chemical manufacturing reached its zenith was Germany and not England. The ambitious chemical industry provided fertile ground for researchers in Germany who were interested in exploring how chemistry affected biology. One of the Germans who had such interests was the legendary Paul Ehrlich.

"Paul Ehrlich was born on 14th March 1854 in Strehlen, Prussia. He was a bookish child. Ehrlich's grandfather had a distillery where the chemical apparatus and setup had a lasting impact on the mind of young Ehrlich. This experience with the distillery laid the foundational bricks for his lifelong love for chemistry. The knowledge and passion for chemistry would become Ehrlich's greatest superpower in the future and help him make discoveries that would change the course of medicine.

"Ehrlich's student years coincided with explosive developments in organic chemistry and unprecedented growth in the development of synthetic dyes. Carl Weigert was Ehrlich's maternal uncle and a dedicated pathologist known for using dyes in medical research. There could not have been a better person than Carl Weigert to inspire Ehrlich to explore the role of dyes in demystifying the microworld of bacterial and human cells.

"One of Ehrlich's first experiments with dyes was feeding a pigeon with a blue colour dye. He anticipated the pigeon to turn blue, but the bird died tragically.

"Ehrlich was interested in medicine, but he never intended to practice it. Medical research appealed to him more than practice. Ehrlich passed his MD exam in 1877 and, the next year, presented his thesis on the staining of blood cells. He reported the discovery of the 'Mast Cell' and inspired others to use Aniline dyes to understand the abnormalities associated with blood cells. This ushered in the birth of 'Haematology'."

Kidnapper: "Could you tell us something about his work on staining bacteria? I guess this work inspired him to use chemicals as 'magic bullets'."

Dr. Parker: "Sure. Bacterial staining has always been a pain in the neck. Staining would revolutionise the study of bacteria, aiding in rapid classification and identification of our microscopic friends and foes. The landmark moment in the world of staining came with the discovery of a highly effective 'Methylene blue' stain. Robert Koch later used the same stain to discover the bacteria that caused Tuberculosis.

"Ehrlich was present during Koch's iconic lecture when he announced the discovery of the Tuberculosis bacteria. Ehrlich later remarked that this was one of the most important moments of his life. Ehrlich accidentally realised that heating the Methylene blue stain made it better and more rapid. The staining method was further improved and is now known as the Ziehl-Neelsen method after the scientists who did the work. Koch was extremely impressed with Ehrlich because of his work in staining TB bacteria, which led to a birth of lifelong admiration for each other. Ehrlich later developed staining techniques for diagnosing typhoid fever using 'Diazo reactions'.

"In 1885, Ehrlich's professor and enthusiastic Patron, Von Frerich, died suddenly. The new head of the department, Carl Gerhardt, was a conventional doctor who was less interested in Ehrlich's research interests. This crisis took a toll on Ehrlich's health, who was diagnosed with Tuberculosis—I guess this was revenge from the Tuberculosis bacteria. He decided to spend some time in the desert of Egypt for a faster recovery and to get over the recent setback with his research setup.

"When Ehrlich returned from Egypt, the only way he could continue with research was by starting a private laboratory. His father-in-law funded the laboratory that was set up at a short distance from his residence.

"With the new research setup, Ehrich started working on new lines of research, including the immune response to plant poisons. He found that mice produced antibodies against poisons like Ricin and Abrin. This new line of investigation resulted in collaboration with Emil Von Behring. Ehrlich also played a significant role towards understanding of active and passive immunity.

---

"In 1897, Ehrlich did his pioneering work on the antigen-antibody interaction. He postulated that the cells that respond to foreign antigens have special receptors to bind with the specific antigens. He called this his 'Side-chain' theory. Ehrlich proposed that chemical affinity made cell receptors and the antibodies stick with each other. Specific chemical interactions were the major driving force behind all the biological activity and function. Chemistry was a key to unraveling the mysteries of biology.

"Ehrlich worked on the antigen-antibody response, and his collaboration with Emil Von Behring led to the successful production of Diphtheria antitoxin. This was a breakthrough against an infectious disease that was a major concern those days. Impressed by these results, the Prussian minister of state established the Institute for Serology and Serum Testing. Ehrlich was appointed as the first director of the institute. This institute in Berlin was fortunately relocated to Frankfurt under the Royal Institute of Experimental Therapy."

Kidnapper: "Why would you call that relocation fortunate? How did the location change help?"

Dr. Parker: "I will make that clear soon.

"Now, let me talk about the birth of chemotherapy. Ehrlich conceived the central idea of chemotherapy while on a return trip to Frankfurt. He asked if dyes could strongly bind to the components of the bacterial cell without harming the innocent cells of humans. What if there was a chemical that had vast differences in terms of its attraction for the bacterial and human cells? Such dyes or chemicals would perfectly qualify as a life-saving drug or 'magic bullet'."

Kidnapper: "I guess Ehrlich's experience working with the stains and antigen-antibody interaction would have helped him develop the fundamental principles of chemotherapy."

Dr. Parker: "Indeed. In both works that you mentioned, the core principle was the attraction of the dyes to the receptors on human cells. It was clear to him that at the cellular level, the boundaries between chemistry and biology blurred. Chemistry was responsible for all biological functions and was the key to ending a lot of human suffering caused by infectious diseases.

"Now, let me talk about the advantage of relocating to Frankfurt."

Kidnapper: "Oh yes. We are waiting for that too."

Dr. Parker: "Sometimes, it is all about being present at a place that offers an unfair advantage. Frankfurt and some other cities in Germany were the headquarters of some of the largest chemical companies in the world. Ehrlich could, therefore, easily procure different chemicals whenever he wanted. He could filter the ones that could be a potential weapon to kill bacteria and other microbes. He also got a large sum to set up his institute of chemotherapy from a wealthy banker's widow in Frankfurt, with Ehrlich himself as its director."

Kidnapper: "A similar advantage was available to Fritz Haber, who made a marriage of Nitrogen and Hydrogen into Ammonia possible. Haber was a German too. His research laboratory was not quite far from BASF, one of the largest chemical makers in the world. Because of this vicinity, the Haber process could be commercialized at such a pace across the globe."

Dr. Parker: "I agree. Ehrlich was lucky to have a flourishing chemical industry around him. He exploited this opportunity and tested as many chemical dyes as possible for their ability to kill bacteria.

"Ehrlich could taste some success with Methylene blue, which he tried as a malaria cure. He was successfully able to cure two malaria patients. However, his new weapon wasn't better than the existing one - Quinine. Ehrlich observed that Methylene blue was less toxic and was strongly attracted to the cells of the malaria-causing parasite. These were the two ideal qualities he expected from a life-saving chemical - a strong affinity for the cells of the parasite and a weaker one for the host cells. Methylene blue was the validation he needed to move further and try other chemicals from the library of available dyes.

"After his mild success with Methylene blue, Ehrlich focused on other protozoal diseases like sleeping sickness. In 1904, Ehrlich and his Japanese colleague Kiyoshi Shiga tested dyes in animals for the sleeping sickness bug *Trypanosoma equine*. Out of hundreds of shades Ehrlich tried, Trypan Red was more successful. The molecule got its name from the colour red and the species of protozoa it killed - *Trypanosoma equine*."

Kidnapper: "Interesting. What about the Salvarsan fame? When did Ehrlich discover that compound? His first magic bullet."

Dr. Parker: "Sure. We are gradually moving towards Salvarsan. However, the road to Salvarsan goes through 'Atoxyl.'"

Kidnapper: "What's that?"

Dr. Parker: "Atoxyl was 'Aminophenyl Arsenic Acid,' an arsenic-based compound that killed the protozoa responsible for the deadly sleeping sickness. Sleeping Sickness is no lesser than a death sentence once contacted. Tsetse flies spread this disease to humans, mainly in a narrow belt in Africa. As the parasite enters the body and multiply, the initial symptoms like fever, headache, joint pains and itching start showing up. Once the microbe crosses the blood brain barrier the disease becomes more sinister. The next stage of symptoms involve changes in behaviour, confusion, difficulty in coordination and speech difficulties. However the most important symptom and the one that makes your life hell is the disturbed sleep cycle. The extreme form of the disease, if left untreated, kills you in a year, while the milder forms keep you alive for some more time. In the absence of treatment as the time passes, you move closer to death for sure.

"The drug Atoxyl was good news as it helped treat sleeping sickness. However, the treatment came with a massive cost."

Kidnapper: "What cost?"

Dr. Parker: "The treatment with Atoxyl was effective only in higher doses, which often led to blindness due to optic nerve damage.

"Ehrlich's success in finding the actual structure of Atoxyl came as a breakthrough here. Ehrlich and Alfred Bertheim showed that Atoxyl was an amino acid derivative of Phenyl Arsenic Acid.

"Since the actual structure of the molecule was known, Ehrlich and his team started playing with it.

They modified the structure of the original compound to get the new chemical siblings. With the modification in the original structure of the molecule, Ehrlich could see a change in their biological effect, too. Based on these observations, he discovered principles that would later lay the foundation for modern medicinal chemistry and drug discovery. Ehrlich realized that even slight modifications in the structure of molecules could drastically affect their biological activity. A wide variety of potent medicines could be synthesized by altering the structures of molecules. The secret sauce of making new medicines was finally revealed. The genie was out of the bottle.

"Meanwhile, in 1905, the culprit behind 'Syphilis' was discovered. Scientists called it '*Treponema pallidium*,' a spiral-shaped bacteria. Fritz Schaudinn and Erich Hoffmann suggested Ehrlich check if some of the chemical weapons in his arsenal also worked against this newly discovered microbe.

"Ehrlich was waiting for Sahachiro Hata."

Kidnapper: "Who was he?"

Dr. Parker: "Hata was Ehrlich's Japanese colleague and student. He had some experience dealing with Syphilis, and Ehrlich considered him the best candidate.

"Hata infected Rabbits with Syphilis and gave them compound 606."

Kidnapper: "Compound 606?"

Dr. Parker: "Ehrlich had made hundreds of new Arsenic compounds with the hope that one of them could become his magic bullet. Compound 606 turned out to be one of them.

"Hata observed that the compound was effective at killing the Syphilis bacteria. Ehrlich and Hata finally demonstrated that chemicals that strongly bind to microbes without harming the host cells could cure deadly diseases. Compound 606, or Arsphenamine, showed that chemistry could help us unlock the doors of human longevity.

"On 19 April 1910, at the Congress of Internal Medicine at Wiesbaden, Ehrlich and Hata presented the discovery of Arsphenamine - a magic bullet to get rid of Syphilis."

Kidnapper: "How was the response to this discovery?"

Dr. Parker: "Ehrlich distributed 65,000 free medicine samples for future testing among humans. The response was phenomenal and a game-changer for Ehrlich. Ehrlich got international recognition and fame for the discovery of Salvarsan. The word 'Salvarsan' came from Arsenic that saves.

"Ehrlich's magic bullets paved the way for a new line of research. The world recognised the hidden and unexplored potential of chemicals in saving lives. Warner Brother Studios produced a feature film titled "Dr. Ehrlich's Magic Bullet" in 1940. Such was the public response to Ehrlich's work in those days. However, Salvarsan wasn't a perfect drug, as it had some side effects. In 1912, the less toxic version of Salvarsan was launched, which was named as 'Neo-Salvarsan.'"

Kidnapper: "Paul Ehrlich single-handedly revolutionised medicine and fathered new fields like haematology, immunology, and chemotherapy. However, more than medicine, his passion for organic chemistry and dyes made him one of the greatest scientists in the history of medicine."

Dr. Parker: "I cannot agree more, Mr. Kidnapper. Anyway, how do you like the content? I hope I could impress you and your students to some extent."

Kidnapper: "What do I say, Dr. Parker? This was out of the world. The history of science is as interesting as the science itself. However, as I said, it is the students who will decide your fate."

Dr. Parker: "My fingers are crossed."

Kidnapper: "Check your WhatsApp, Dr. Parker."

Dr. Parker: "What? Just a 50% satisfaction rate. I tried my best to engage students. Weren't you impressed?"

Kidnapper: "I was impressed, but I believe your language was tough for the students to understand. Bad luck, Dr. Parker. You will not get any clues to reach Rachit this time.

"You should also try to be more entertaining."

Dr. Parker: "Entertaining? You have kidnapped my son, and you want me to entertain you?"

Kidnapper: "Ok. Do as you want to? Do you not love your son anymore?"

Dr. Parker: "Ok…bring it on? Ask me the next question."

Kidnapper: "What are your views on the term 'drug,' Dr. Parker?"

Dr. Parker: "For the layman, drugs are all about habit-forming narcotic chemicals. If you go to a common man and ask him if he has taken a drug, you might get slapped badly. However, the word "Drug" has a broader meaning. Drugs are chemicals that produce a physiological or psychological change in the body when taken. For example, the drugs could lower your blood pressure or decrease the acid secretion in your stomach, while some of them could help you control your anxiety attack.

"The drugs that can cure a disease are classified as "Medicine." The one that harms or leads to an unfavourable response is classified as 'Poison'.

"The same drug used as medicine could become poison in higher doses. It is all about the correct quantity.

"Heath Ledger, who played the iconic character of 'Joker' in Christopher Nolan's movie 'The Dark Knight,' died from a drug overdose of prescription medicine. Overdose of painkillers is also one of the most common causes of liver failure in the US."

Kidnapper: "Could you shed some light on the classification of the drugs?"

Dr. Parker: "Sure. You can use the following code if you wish to remember all the categories of drug classification. It is P.B.S.T. When learning complex things, it is better to make a 'mnemonic' that is easy to recall. The first letter of each word shall indicate the word to be remembered. You can create a sentence like Please Be serious Tom, where P will help you remember Pharmacological, B is for Biochemical and S from serious will help you remember Structure. Lastly, T from Tom will help you remember target. I suggest making funny statements that are easy to recall.

"The following are the different classifications of drugs:

"P - Pharmacological

B - Biochemical

S - Structure

T - Target"

Kidnapper: "Would you please elaborate on some of the classifications?"

Dr. Parker: "The Pharmacological classification is widely used by doctors. This classification is based on what the drug does to the body. For example, the drugs that provide pain relief are called analgesics. The word 'analgesia' has a Greek origin. It is derived from the Greek words 'an'-meaning 'without' and 'algesis' which means 'sense of pain.' Thus, 'analgesia' translates to 'without pain'.

"The drugs that lower blood pressure are called 'Antihypertensive.' Similarly, some drugs decrease glucose in the blood. The doctors call them oral hypoglycemics. Hypo means low and glycemic index indicates sugar levels in the blood.

"The structure-based classification is simple. Many drugs with similar functions have a similar chemical structure or backbone. The drugs could be considered 'chemical siblings.' These drugs belong to the same family of molecules and, therefore, also show similar effects on the body. The example often mentioned in the books is the family of medicines called 'Sulphonamides'.

"Every medicine prescribed by doctors binds to a particular target. The last classification is based on the targets that the drugs attach to. These drug targets could be made of proteins like enzymes, ion gates, and cellular receptors. The targets could also be composed of carbohydrates and lipids like those in bacterial cell walls. Finally, the drugs could also directly bind to genetic material like DNA. For example, drugs that kill cancer cells directly attach to their DNA and interfere with the cell division."

Kidnapper: "Dr. Parker, could you tell us something about the working mechanism of drugs that bind to enzymes?"

Dr. Parker: "It is impossible for any life on this planet to survive without their specific enzymes. It might surprise you to learn that the slowest biological process could take one trillion years to complete in the absence of the enzymes. Enzymes are highly efficient in carrying out the biological processes.

"One important trait of enzymes is their loyalty."

Kidnapper: "Loyal as in?"

Dr. Parker: "They stay with one specific substrate all their life.

"Let me help you with examples. The Urease enzyme helps break down Urea, while the lactase enzyme helps digest lactose sugar, and so on. You cannot eat grass like cattle as your body does not produce 'cellulase' enzyme."

Kidnapper: "What if we insert a gene in humans that codes for cellulase enzymes?"

Dr. Parker: "In that case, you might find people adding grass to their green salad and eating it happily."

Kidnapper: "Really?"

Dr. Parker: "I am kidding. It is not that easy for humans to digest grass. You need more than the cellulase enzyme to do that. A whole set of collective changes across the digestive system would be needed to make humans eat grass.

"Enzymes are among the most common targets for drugs. There are many drugs used by humans that target enzymes. For example, Lipitor was among the world's best-selling medications for a long time. The drug blocks an important enzyme that helps produce 'Cholesterol.' Therefore, the medication is prescribed to prevent heart attacks and brain strokes. Similarly, the drugs given to HIV patients target the essential enzymes that help HIV in making its baby viruses. These antiviral molecules block enzymes like proteases and reverse transcriptase, which are important for the virus to continue its life cycle.

"Understanding the 3D structure of essential enzymes and creating or finding molecules that could block them has helped pharmaceutical companies launch medicines for diseases that were not curable earlier. Of course, the companies—the giant ones—have made billions of dollars in the course of doing this."

Kidnapper: "Now, let's discuss the specific drugs mentioned in the textbook. Let's start with the Antacids."

Dr. Parker: "Antacids mean 'Anti-acids.' These drugs either neutralize the excessive acid or stop its production in the stomach.

"There are two ways to cure acidity. You can reduce the acid's production or neutralize the excessive acid using a basic or an alkaline solution.

"Chemical messengers called histamines are responsible for releasing acid into your stomach. Histamines are key to the lock of the gates of acid factories in your stomach. The blocker and the original molecule are like chemical twins. The blockers fool the receptors into believing that they are the original molecules. They take the spot of the original molecule and prevent its attachment further. Cimetidine and Ranitidine are examples of histamine blockers used to prevent acid secretion in the stomach.

"Another category of drugs used in the treatment of acidity is the one that blocks the 'proton pumps.' But why are they called (Proton pumps)? The acidity of any solution is measured in terms of hydrogen ion concentration in a solution.

"What is left after you remove an electron from a hydrogen atom?"

Kidnapper: "A proton?"

Dr. Parker: "Right. For this reason, the Hydrogen ion is considered a proton, and the pump controlling its movement is called a proton pump. The process of acid release in the stomach is regulated by the ion channels managed by a molecular pump called the $H^+/K^+$ ATPase pump. These tiny molecular machines control the flow of protons and, hence, acid production in the stomach. The drugs that block these pumps are called 'Proton-pump inhibitors.' Medications like 'lansoprazole and pantoprazole' are the most common examples of this category."

Kidnapper: "So if antihistamines are the duplicate keys that block the lock of gates of an acid factory, then using the proton-pump inhibitors is equivalent to shutting the factory itself."

Dr. Parker: "Exactly."

Kidnapper: "You could also cure acidity by neutralising the extra acid in the stomach using basic solutions. 'Alkaline solutions' containing sodium bicarbonate, magnesium hydroxide, and aluminium hydroxide solutions are most widely used in the antacids."

Kidnapper: "Is it true that excessive acidity can cause ulcers and that most ulcers are induced by stress?"

Dr. Parker: "Stress as a cause of ulcers is an old theory. This perception about the mechanism of ulceration changed completely after a remarkable, daring act by an Australian Doctor named Dr. Barry Marshall."

Kidnapper: "I have never heard of that name, but I want to learn about his story."

Dr. Parker: "Dr. Marshall was born in Kalgoorlie, a town famous for gold mining located some 400 miles east of Perth, Australia. His dad fixed steam engines and trains, whereas his mom was a nurse. Barry had many books around him as a kid on mechanical engineering, chemistry, electricity and biology. Young Barry was deeply curious about the world around him, and the environment at home fuelled the fire of his curiosity further.

"As part of his internal medicine training, Dr. Barry Marshall was required to undertake a research project. And guess what?"

Kidnapper: "What?"

Dr. Parker: "Well, Dr. Marshall took on a Nobel Prize-winning project. Marshall's boss told him to meet hospital pathologist Dr. Warren, who was studying the tissue samples of patients with stomach ulcers and cancer.

"Dr. Robin Warren had discovered an interesting bacterium in the biopsy samples of ulcer and stomach cancer patients. He wanted someone to assist him and discover who this new member of the bacterial family was and how it managed to live in one of the most hostile places in the human body."

Kidnapper: "What bacterium?"

Dr. Parker: "While analyzing tissue samples from ulcer and stomach cancer patients, Dr. Warren found attractive S-shaped or helical bacteria. He consistently found the same microbe in the stomach tissue samples of the ulcer patients, too. Dr. Warren convinced Dr. Marshall to check if he could find something more.

"The stomach is not a great place to live in a human body. In those days, people could not imagine bacteria living peacefully in the stomach as the environment was too acidic for any microbial life to survive. Dr. Marshall got excited about the possibility of finding a new bacterium that was daring enough to take this challenge and swim against the tide of acid."

Kidnapper: "What an exciting opportunity to learn something new about the human body and its conditions."

Dr. Parker: "Indeed.

"Dr. Warren gave a list of patients to Dr. Marshall and asked him to find the source of these infections. Dr. Marshall surprisingly found a patient's name on the list, whom he knew personally. She had come up with stomach pain but was referred to the psychiatric department later as they could not link the pain to anything. Another of his Russian patients recovered from stomach pain after he completed his course of antibiotics. Somehow, these things made Dr. Marshall investigate the real cause of the ulcer and see if there was any link between ulcers and the mysterious stomach bacteria. Dr. Barry Marshall decided to check the presence of the bacteria among some 100 patients with a history of duodenal ulcers. The duodenum is your entry point to the long tube of the small intestine.

"To prove the link between the bacterium *Helicobacter pylori* and ulcers, it was important to isolate and grow the bacteria from the tissue samples of ulcer patients. Dr. Marshall got a local microbiology expert to join his team and do the relevant work.

"The lab technicians tended to throw the bacterial culture plates the next day if they did not see any bacteria growing. Unfortunately, they could not find anything for the first 30 patients. However, the microbiologist called Dr. Marshall one day and informed him about the coatings of *Helicobacter pylori* bacteria in the culture plates linked to the duodenal ulcer patients. The team observed that *Helicobacter pylori* was a slow-growing bacteria that took 3 days to grow and form a coat. All of the duodenal ulcer patients had *Helicobacter pylori* infection and Dr. Marshall considered this much more than a coincidence. The stomach cancer patients, too, had developed gastritis in the background."

Kidnapper: "Okay, this study provided the most substantial evidence to prove that *Helicobacter pylori* was the real culprit behind the ulcers."

Dr. Parker: "You cannot defame a bacterium without strong evidence. If you associate their name with a disease they do not cause, they might file a defamation lawsuit."

Kidnapper: "Lol."

Dr. Parker: "We have a history of not immediately accepting new ideas. For the world to take their research seriously, it was important for Dr. Marshall and Dr. Warren to infect animals and follow the symptoms they developed further."

Kidnapper: "You mean an animal model of the disease was important?"

Dr. Parker: "Exactly. An animal model.

"Dr. Marshall tried to infect some pigs with the bacteria to check if they got ulcers, too. However, he failed. Also, the piglets grew into large pigs rapidly, which created budget issues. At this juncture, he decided to drink the bacteria culture himself.

"Dr. Marshall checked to see if he had any bacteria in his stomach. Once he got the results, he decided to drink the culture and conduct one of the most famous and iconic self-experiments in the history of medicine."

Kidnapper: "He drank the culture?"

Dr. Parker: "Of course, he drank the bacteria culture. Dr. Marshall developed gastritis in the next 5 days. His wife found out about his self-experiment from the bad breath he had developed from the infection. Along with the ethics committee, getting approval from the boss at home was equally important. His wife wasn't happy with him and feared that the kids would get infected, too."

Kidnapper: "What about gastritis? Did he develop that too?"

Dr. Parker: "Yes, he did. The biopsy of his stomach confirmed the heavy coating of the spiral bacteria in the stomach."

Kidnapper: "I am sure this evidence would have convinced the world about the role of *Helicobacter pylori* in causing ulcers."

Dr. Parker: "I wish things were this simple. Some of the world's most significant truths have faced the most fierce resistance from the lobbyists of dogma. Some examples are Einstein's hypothesis on the particle nature of light and Darwin's claim on our relation with apes. Although apes feel offended by our claim that we are relatives.

"The research papers that Dr. Robin Warren and Dr. Barry Marshall wrote on the *Helicobacter pylori* and ulcer connection were rejected by the famous journal 'The Lancet'. The duo knew that they were on the verge of making a landmark discovery, so they presented their work at a conference in Brussels. They faced fewer skeptical eyes for their idea in Brussels, though."

Kidnapper: "So, what was the most significant impact of this work?"

Dr. Parker: "Earlier, gastric ulcers were treated with antacids, antihistamines, and proton-pump inhibitors.

This was because stress, spicy food, and lifestyle changes were considered the main factors that caused ulcers. Pharma companies made billions of dollars selling expensive acidity medicines. However, these tablets never cured ulcers. The disease would return most of the time if the medicines were discontinued.

"There were also a large number of patients who underwent surgery to get rid of their ulcers. However, the surgery made their life hell most of the time. On the other hand, the antibiotic approach was more effective in treating ulcers as it targeted the root cause - the bacteria. The treatment of *Helicobacter pylori* infection with antibiotics has significantly reduced stomach cancer cases in the Western world. However, one must remember that only some people who have *Helicobacter pylori* in their stomachs get ulcers. These bacteria seem innocent passengers within the human gut and use it as their rented home. The majority of humans carry these bacteria, and not all of them complain of ulcers. There is something that disturbs the equilibrium in your gut and leads to ulcers."

Kidnapper: "My students have a question about how this bacteria survives in the stomach's highly acidic environment."

Dr. Parker: "This is a highly educated bacteria that knows about acid-base reactions. It produces an enzyme called Urease that breaks down Urea into Ammonia and Carbon dioxide. Ammonia is basic, and it neutralises the acid in the bacteria's surroundings so that it can exist peacefully. The bacteria also move to the layers of the stomach that are comparatively less acidic."

Kidnapper: "Smart bacteria. Why is it called *Helicobacter pylori* ?"

Dr. Parker: "As we have discussed, it is an S-shaped helical bacteria and hence called "Helicobacter." On the other hand, the meaning of Pylorus in Greek is 'Gatekeeper.' The region is a gatekeeper between the food that moves from the stomach to the small intestine. It is also less acidic than the other stomach regions, making it a better home choice for the bacteria.

"This story of Dr. Warren and Dr. Marshall offers important lessons about how science should be done."

Kidnapper: "I am sure there are many."

Dr. Parker: "This story has lessons about doing great science. You would find two qualities among scientists who are known for breaking new ground in the world of scientific research. You can see those qualities in Dr. Robin Warren and Dr. Barry Marshall.

"The qualities I am talking about are 'courage and open-mindedness'.

"More than intelligence, traits like courage could take you to great heights in science."

Kidnapper: "Ahh…I see. You must believe in yourself even when the world thinks you are a fool. You must take risks in proposing specific ideas even if they threaten the current scientific establishment."

Dr. Parker: "Yup. If you have evidence backing up your claims and have tried your best to prove yourself wrong. Let me quote Carl Sagan here to make my point."

**"Science is based on experiment, on a willingness to challenge old dogma, on an openness to see the universe as it is. Accordingly, science sometimes requires courage - at least the courage to question conventional wisdom."**

"Paul Dirac also made an interesting statement on how scientific progress should be measured:"

**"Scientific progress is measured in units of courage, not intelligence."**

"For example, Einstein dared to challenge the long-held "wave nature of light." It took more than 16 years for the world to take Einstein and his particle nature of light, i.e., light quanta, seriously. Darwin had to face similar hurdles in making the world accept his theory, which took away the special status of humans forever. Then there are people like Galileo who was persecuted for telling the truth.

"Dr. Marshall showed enormous courage by challenging the long-held dogma that stress causes ulcer. His work paved the way for a new type of thinking. He ensured that microbes were given equal weightage while we tried to demystify the cause of chronic diseases. As of now, more than 20% of cancers worldwide are linked to microbes. Do you know what this means to the world?"

Kidnapper: "I am not sure."

Dr. Parker: "This means that antibiotics and vaccines can prevent a large number of cancers. Cervarix is one such example—it is a vaccine that has been launched to prevent cancers caused by the Human Papilloma Virus—the microbial villain infamous for causing more than 70% of cervical cancer cases. The vaccine is a great step forward in terms of reducing this cancer."

Kidnapper: "I found this story interesting. Let me check for the polls and share them with you."

"Check your WhatsApp, Dr. Parker."

Dr. Parker had no idea how his answer would impact the invisible students controlling his fate. Dr. Parker opened the message and smiled when he saw that number, 85%. The poll results also came up with the instructions to locate Rachit: "Take 3000 steps straight. Now remember that by the end of those 3000 steps you will come across 2 large trees. One would be on your left side while another would be on your right. Both the trees are linked to 2 different routes and only one of them would take you to Rachit. You will notice that the trees have the names of European cities written on them. The tree that would take you to Rachit is linked to a city where one of the greatest physicists was born. This physicist played a significant role to convince the world that atoms are real and they must be taken seriously. To get the next round of questions and clue to reach Rachit you must take 1000 steps further along the path starting from the tree you chose. Only when you have walked those 1000 steps that you would hear my voice again for the next question. I would also let you know if you have chosen a wrong tree and hence you will have to come back again and take the right path.

I am sure you know that this would waste lots of your time. Choose wisely. Best of luck."

Dr. Parker took those 3000 steps and found 2 giant trees right in front of him that were followed by two different routes. He started scanning the right tree from top to bottom after getting a bit closer. He could see those 3 alphabets 'U, L, and M' written one beneath the other. Dr. Parker had read a lot about Albert Einstein, and hence he knew that 'Ulm' was Einstein's birthplace. Dr. Parker started running along the path of this tree as fast as he could. The moment he completed his 1000 steps, he heard that strange voice again.

Kidnapper: "Well played, Dr. Parker! You did not even bother to check what was written on the tree to your left."

Dr. Parker: "I know I am running out of time. And it wasn't difficult for me to guess that you were talking about Albert Einstein."

Kidnapper: "I am impressed. Now let us come to the next category of drugs, Dr. Parker. Let us talk about the antihistamines used to treat allergies and coughs."

Dr. Parker: "Oh yes. I hope you know how allergies feel. Be it itching, sneezing, or watery eyes, histamines should be held responsible for all those symptoms. What should you do in that case? Simple: Block the action of histamine.

"Antihistamines like Brompheniramine and Terfenadine are used to treat coughs and allergies.

"I have dinosaurs jumping in my stomach. I am feeling tired and hungry. Can I get some food?"

Kidnapper: "Sure, Dr. Parker. We need you alive. So don't worry. We have all the arrangements for you. However, there is a slight twist here."

Dr. Parker: "What twist? Aren't your questions enough?"

Kidnapper: "The food we will send you is a puzzle in itself. Every food item is inspired by a scientist and his discovery. You will have to guess the scientist based on your experiences with the dish. You will get your food in 5 minutes."

Dr. Parker could see a trolley coming towards him. The smell of his favourite food caused his mouth to become full of saliva. Dr. Parker's eyes twinkled to find some of his favourite dishes as the trolley approached him. The smell of the food made him travel back in time. It reminded him of his beloved mom, who used to make food with deep warmth and love for her only child. Mom's dahi-vada had a fan following. She used to soak the menduvadas in the night. In the morning, she would pour curd on them. She would then sprinkle some spices on it, including cinnamon powder, red chilli powder, and salt. She would then add coriander leaves for garnishing. The result used to be one of the best dahi-vada in the world. Relatives would flock to the kite-flying festival and Holi to try delicacies Dr. Parker's mom made. What made her dishes special was her love to feed others. She believed that making people happy through food was equivalent to feeding God himself.

The thoughts about his favourite childhood dishes had taken over Dr. Parker's mind.

Kidnapper: "Time has stopped for you, Dr. Parker."

The kidnapper's voice made Dr. Parker alert again.

Dr. Parker relished every dish he saw and ate to the fullest.

Kidnapper: "How was the food?"

Dr. Parker: "It was amazing. Thank you very much for this kind gesture. I had a chance to live my childhood again. I felt as if mom had sent this all to me."

Kidnapper: "Great. Are you ready for the food-based questions?"

Dr. Parker: "Yes, I am ready."

Kidnapper: "Here are the questions for you. These are mostly the dishes that your mom did not cook. The quiz shall get easy in that case. Here is your first question:

"Which of the following scientists would you associate the chocolate brownie with?

"Your options are:

A. Albert Einstein   B. Werner Heisenberg   C. Niels Bohr   D. Wolfgang Pauli

Dr. Parker: "D. Wolfgang Pauli."

Kidnapper: "That's quick. Would you care to explain?"

Dr. Parker: "Oh yes. I love chocolate brownies. I wanted to eat as much as possible. However, I observed that I could not eat more than 2, even though the brownie was the first thing I tried. And that's something strange. How could you eat only 2 brownies with an empty stomach when you can eat many? It is only possible if there is some inherent limit to how much you can eat.

"Since I could not eat more than 2 brownies, this could be compared to Pauli's exclusion principle, which limits the number of electrons an orbital can accommodate. According to Pauli's famous exclusion principle, an orbital cannot have more than 2 electrons. It must be called a 'Pauli Brownie.'"

Kidnapper: "That's amazing. What about the 'Suji ka halwa'?"

Dr. Parker: "It looked like 'Suji ka halwa,' but I could simultaneously feel the taste of halwa and upma. It was extraordinary, but I felt this way. It looked like the halwa simultaneously had the dual nature of halwa and upma. I would, therefore, call it the 'Broglie' halwa due to its similarity with the dual nature of matter particles as proposed by the French scientist Louis de Broglie."

Kidnapper: "Impressive. Any comments on the Mango thick shake?"

Dr. Parker: "Hmmm, I never had anything colder than the Mango thick shake in my life. I felt like it must be the coldest thing I could ever tolerate. I would, therefore, compare the Mango thick shake with 'Bose-Einstein condensate.' I could hardly take one sip."

Kidnapper: "Interesting. What about pizza? And this is the most important question for you. You would badly screw up if you got this one wrong."

Dr. Parker: "I have not been happier in my life. The pizza was amazing."

What scientist could be connected to this? Dr. Parker started thinking hard. He started biting his nails again.

He also started walking to clear his thinking as the stakes were high.

Dr. Parker: "I don't think the pizza was related to any scientist. I think the cheese added to the pizza was loaded with a large amount of dopamine. Otherwise, how could I feel so happy?"

Kidnapper: "Isn't that level of happiness a natural response when you eat pizza? I mean, don't we get euphoric after eating our favourite pizzas?

"Anyways,

Dr. Parker, now we would like to know about the neurologically active drugs."

Dr. Parker: "Neurologically active drugs cross a special barricade in your brain known as the blood-brain barrier and target the specific receptors present there. These drugs are used for different types of mental illness and to manage pain.

"The most important category of neurologically active drugs mentioned in the textbook is tranqilisers. This category of drugs calms your mind and helps deal with the feeling of excessive excitation, anxiety, and stress.

"Reserpine was among the first tranqilisers that humans identified. It was known to calm the animals it was given to."

Kidnapper: "Dr. Parker, please tell us how these medicines work."

Dr. Parker: "Sure. Before that, I would like to tell you a story.

"I would talk about drugs that enter the brain and alter our emotions, for sure. However, you would be surprised to learn about certain parasites that hijack the brains of a host for their advantage—parasites that make their hosts dance to their tune."

Kidnapper: "Hijack the brain? A parasite? That's quite a difficult task."

Dr. Parker: "It is. Let me share the details here.

"Let me talk about a genius parasite that plays with his host's mind to achieve its ultimate biological goal."

Kidnapper: "I am still not getting this. How can a tiny parasite hijack someone's mind?"

Dr. Parker: "Survive and send your genes to the next generation. This is the most important goal of any biological organism that has ever taken birth on this planet - this applies to those gigantic dinosaurs that ruled this planet once to the microscopic viruses."

Kidnapper: "Of course. You have told me this before."

Dr. Parker: "Cool. I was checking to see if you were attentive enough during our conversation. The name of this brain manipulator parasite is *Toxoplasma gondii.*"

Kidnapper: "But why would a parasite manipulate its host? What is the parasite trying to achieve by playing with the host's mind?"

Dr. Parker: "The parasite's problem is that it has certain limitations regarding how and where it can reproduce."

Kidnapper: "What limitations?"

Dr. Parker: "This parasite can only reproduce inside the stomach of cats. It must reach the cat's gut at any cost to complete its life cycle. Only in the cat's stomach *Toxoplasma gondii* successfully form Oocysts. Oocysts are structures that contain the infective particles of the parasite. They are stable in the external environment and can contaminate water, soil, and food to move from one host to another. These microbes must find ways to infect new cats to continue the chain of infection, or they risk becoming extinct.

"*Toxoplasma gondii* has found a way to achieve this goal of reaching cats via an intermediate host."

Kidnapper: "Now, what's an intermediate host?"

Dr. Parker: "As the name suggests, an intermediate host is not the main host. Instead, the intermediate host is a means to reach the target or main host."

Kidnapper: "What's the intermediate host in this case?"

Dr. Parker: "The intermediate host is the mice.

"You know that mice are one of the essential items on cats' dinner menus.

"Cats love eating them without adding mayonnaise or sauce."

Kidnapper: "Lol....of course, I know that."

Dr. Parker: "You would agree that mice must have developed their defence mechanisms against the cats."

Kidnapper: "I am sure."

Dr. Parker: "The mice can sniff the urine of cats and run away instantly. The smell of a cat is equivalent to inviting death for them.

"The fear among the mice for the cats has been helping them to escape the clutches of death many times. It is a psychological defence that's a lifesaver for the mice.

"However, things turn out differently when the mice are infected with *Toxoplasma gondii*."

Kidnapper: "How?"

Dr. Parker: "We know by research that mice infected with the parasite *Toxoplasma gondii* suddenly become brave. They become daring enough to face the cats and lose their inherent fear.

"*Toxoplasma gondii* present in the brain of mice brings this dramatic shift in the personality of mice. The parasite does this magic by playing with the mice's Amygdala."

Kidnapper: "Isn't that the centre of emotions in our brain, too?"

Dr. Parker: "Indeed. The parasite turns off the switch of fear in the mice so the cat can quickly eat them."

Kidnapper: "Wow. So, the parasite affects the region of the brain that controls emotion."

Dr. Parker: "Yes. The parasite infects the mice's Amygdala, a region known to process emotional responses such as fear."

Kidnapper: "Does this manipulation or the infection of mice's Amygdala also affect their fear of other things?"

Dr. Parker: "Now, that's a fascinating question. Unlike cat urine, mice's response to dog urine is unaffected. In short, the manipulation by *Toxoplasma gondii* is highly specific and limited to interactions with cats—the ultimate hosts for the parasites. However, the most surprising element of this parasite is its ability to attract mice to cat urine."

Kidnapper: "This is such a fatal attraction—the attraction to death."

Dr. Parker: "It is for sure.

"The infection of *Toxoplasma gondii* causes the mice to indulge in risky behaviours, making them easy prey for the cat. Once the mice are eaten, the cunning parasites enter the cat's gut, where they reproduce to continue their eternal duty of sending the genes to the next generation."

Kidnapper: "Thank god this parasite does not infect humans. Imagine if a bug like this made us attracted to lions or tigers."

Dr. Parker: "In that case, lions and tigers would party daily.

"By the way, this parasite does infect humans."

Kidnapper: "What? Are you serious? Is that why we find cats cute? And does it similarly affect our brains?"

Dr. Parker: "The effect on our brains is not as intense as in mice. However, research says that people with *Toxoplasma gondii* in their brains indulge more in risky behaviours than uninfected people."

Kidnapper: "The infection should also be shared among business people. I mean the entrepreneurs."

Dr. Parker: "Omg... how do you know that?"

Kidnapper: "Isn't that obvious? Entrepreneurs take massive risks in their lives to establish their businesses.

Their risk-taking appetite separates courageous entrepreneurs from others."

Dr. Parker: "I read a research paper in which they found that students infected with *Toxoplasma gondii* had higher chances of becoming entrepreneurs than others. You guessed it right. But it is also known that more than 35% of the human population is already infected with this genius parasite. Hence, what we think of as causation could also be a correlation.

"We would need more in-depth studies to prove the role of *Toxoplasma gondii* in risk-taking behaviour among humans. A more extensive study is required to establish this exciting relationship between the Toxoplasma infection and Elon Musk-type qualities."

Kidnapper: "Wow. This was out of this world, Dr. Parker. Who would have thought parasites with a single cell could control organisms with billions and trillions of cells? It is all about who is running faster on the treadmill of evolution."

Dr. Parker: "Wow, that's a nice way to express that sentiment. Let me come to the tranqilisers.

"In 1957, scientists working with a pharma company's research and development department found a compound that could reduce the emotion of 'fear' among animals. The drug was named 'Librium.' The same drug was also found to decrease anxiety among humans. So, a lot of drugs with a similar tranquilising effect were manufactured by modifying the structure of the primary molecule. When given Librium, mice could show the courage to fight cats directly as we saw in the case of the *Toxoplasma gondii* infection. The mice die eventually, but they would not fear death before taking that action."

Kidnapper: "Yeah. Jerry has often done this to Tom in the famous Tom and Jerry Show. I believe Jerry, the mouse, was always on tranquilisers or had that microbe playing with his mind."

Dr. Parker: "By the way, do you know the meaning of the word 'Tranquillity ?"

Kidnapper: "I don't know."

Dr. Parker: "The word comes from the Latin term 'tranquillitas,' which means calmness or peace."

Kidnapper: "I know that these drugs, once taken, make you calm and peaceful. Doctors prescribe this medicine to patients who have anxiety issues. I am interested in the working mechanism of the medicine Dr. Parker. How do these medicines exactly calm your mind? What exactly do they do to your brain to achieve this effect?"

Dr. Parker: "The tranquilisers make it difficult for your neurons to fire their electrical signals. In short, they reduce the generation of electrical activity among the neurons."

Kidnapper: "I guess now it is time to discuss the antidepressants. Would you like to shed some light on their mechanism, Dr. Parker?"

Dr. Parker: "Sure. Before I discuss the mechanism of antidepressants, I must talk about the role of molecules called neurotransmitters that help in the expression of mood and emotion. You might have heard of molecules like Dopamine, Oxytocin, Serotonin, and

Norepinephrine. Dopamine is famously called the 'pleasure' or the 'feel-good' molecule, which I will soon prove to be a misconception."

Kidnapper: "Please wait, Dr. Parker."

Dr. Parker: "Why? What happened?"

Kidnapper: "We have a question coming from one of our students. He wants to know what decides if something will make us happy or cause pain. Is there any biological algorithm with pre-defined rules about what would make us happy and sad?"

Dr. Parker: "Wow. I must say that your students are brilliant. This is an interesting question; to answer it, I must go back to our evolutionary past. As in biology, all that you see in the present is the result of how you overcame the survival and reproductive challenges in the past."

Kidnapper: "Sure. Take us wherever you want to. Just ensure that you satisfy the curiosity of our students."

Dr. Parker: "Surely, I will. Anything that helps us survive and reproduce would give us immense pleasure, while things that threaten our survival or ability to transfer our genes are painful.

"Let me explain this with some examples.

"Have you ever wondered why kids are so fond of food that tastes sweet? Forget the kids, for that matter. Even as adults, we love eating chocolate, ice creams, and a long list of sugar-rich foods."

Kidnapper: "You mean eating sugar feels good because it helped our ancestors survive in some way?"

Dr. Parker: "Exactly. Sugars are energy-rich, and eating them would have helped our ancestors get the calories they needed to survive the day."

Kidnapper: "Wow. It makes complete sense to make eating sugar so pleasant. It led to our survival and helped us identify foods rich in energy."

Dr. Parker: "You got the point. I am sure it is not difficult to guess the opposite."

Kidnapper: "Opposite?"

Dr. Parker: "I would like to ask your brilliant students if they could try to explain the evolution of bitter taste. How would it have helped our ancestors survive better?"

Kidnapper: "This is an interesting question, for sure. I would love to challenge my students on this. You will soon get an answer."

Dr. Parker: "Sure. I am waiting."

Kidnapper: "I got the answer, Dr. Parker. One of my students is saying that bitterness is an unpleasant feeling. It might have evolved for us to avoid certain types of food. This is in contrast to the sweet taste, which encourages us to eat things like sugar that are rich in energy. The bitter taste is all about avoiding certain types of food that might harm us somehow."

Dr. Parker: "Wow. I am impressed. Your students have gotten to the core of how biology works. Indeed, many things in our evolutionary history would kill us if we ate them. The bitter taste evolved to help us avoid anything that could be poisonous or threaten our survival."

Kidnapper: "I guess we could also explain the feeling of disgust based on this logic. There is a reason why we feel disgusted by faecal material, garbage, or filth around us. Spoiled food smells so bad, and so does rotten meat.

"Imagine if you have lost your sense of smell and cannot identify if your food is not fresh enough. It smells bad, but your senses are not working. If you eat that food, you will soon visit a doctor for a serious stomach infection. Similarly, the cue of smell that helped us judge if the food was healthy enough for us had a major survival advantage for our ancestors. It protected us from eating or coming in contact with anything that was a potential source of infection."

Dr. Parker: "Wow, Mr. Kidnapper. Not bad. You have started to think like Charles Darwin."

Kidnapper: "Thanks for the compliment. But remember, we are not friends. I have kidnapped your son, and it is you who shall enchant and educate my students, not me. Let us continue with the topic of dopamine again."

Dr. Parker: "Of course.

"Dopamine is not only about pleasure. Research has shown that the maximum amount of dopamine is released when we are surprised in a positive way. Let me give you an example to explain this point. I visited Switzerland for a conference recently. Before the event, I used to imagine what my experience could be. The prospect of exploring one of the countries top in my bucket list, and that too for a scientific purpose, made me very happy. I had never been more excited in my life. When I reached there, the first thing I did was visit Einstein's home. Einstein, like many others, has been my childhood hero, too. It was a dream to visit his house in Bern and go back in time to imagine how Einstein would have derived the equations that changed the course of physics forever. The experience was out of this universe. I had never been so happy. The reason was the fact that this trip turned out even better than I had imagined. This was a positive surprise. This is when your brain rewards you with dopamine most. In short, dopamine is a molecule of surprise and exploration. It makes you explore things and be excited about the future.

"Dopamine is also released when we find something new. For this reason, modern humans feel good when they learn something new, be it a fact or a skill. Dopamine is also responsible for most creative pursuits. Dopamine helps us connect knowledge from diverse domains and create something new. From Picasso to J.K. Rowling, all the creative geniuses might have brains loaded with extra dopamine.

"Dopamine possibly helped humans to conquer the world by being more adventurous and brave. When humans were exploring uncharted terrains around them, taking risks and being adventurous might have paid off well. Thanks to dopamine again."

Kidnapper: "Cool. Now, please come to the mechanism of the antidepressants."

Dr. Parker: "You see, antidepressants were discovered accidentally. Nature has surprising ways of revealing profound truths to people who are passionately curious.

"Iproniazid, the first modern antidepressant was originally a drug given to the patients of tuberculosis. However the doctors observed that tuberculosis patients taking iproniazid had interesting side-effects like better moods, appetite and sleep. These were considered side-effects because these mood enhancing effect of iproniazid was not consistent across the patients. The scientists later conducted systematic clinical trials to check the role of iproniazid among the patients of clinical depression. The medicine was given to the patients of depression for many weeks and the researchers found improvement among 70% of the patients."

Kidnapper: "This is such a beautiful example of serendipity in science. When it comes to science, fortune favours the curious. I would love to know the mechanism of these antidepressants."

Dr. Parker: "Sure. The expression of mood in the brain happens through the release of special chemical messengers. Since these chemicals contain one amino group directly linked to an aromatic ring, they are called monoamines. The most common mood regulating monoamine neurotransmitters are serotonin, dopamine and norepinephrine. As per one of the theories, depression results from the imbalance of these mood regulating chemicals. So if we could control the production, expression and destruction of these chemicals, we could also control mood of an individual.

"Once these mood-regulating chemicals like dopamine, serotonin, and norepinephrine are released in the gap between the two neurons called the synaptic cleft, they are either taken back through the reuptake mechanism or destroyed after they are done with their job. So, many antidepressant medicines work by tweaking these two different mechanisms. There are also other mechanisms through which the antidepressants manifest their effect.

"Enzymes destroy the monoamines once these chemical messengers have accomplished their mission. Some antidepressant medicines interfere with or block the activity of these enzymes that destroy the mood-regulating chemicals. This leads to the circulation of the neurotransmitters in the synaptic cleft for a longer time and helps those with depression.

"The mood-regulating neurotransmitters are kept in molecular packets called vesicles before being released in the space between two neurons. Consider these chemical messengers as the key to a lock of good mood. The keys must open the locks present on the neurons on the other side. We call these locks 'receptors'. The neurotransmitters are stored back in tiny molecular packets to avoid continuous stimulation. This can be called molecular recycling of mood-controlling chemicals or the 'reuptake mechanism,' as I just mentioned. What certain antidepressant drugs do is that they do not let this reuptake happen. This makes the chemical messengers linger more between the neurons and provide some relief to the patients of depression. One of the most widely used antidepressants, named 'Prozac,' is known to block the reuptake of serotonin."

Kidnapper: "Is it true that this theory of monoamine imbalance as the cause of depression has limitations? I recently learned that these medicines take at least a week to show their effects. Depression isn't all about the imbalance of monoamines it seems."

Dr. Parker: "You are right. Indeed, the mood-enhancing effects of these medicines are not immediate.

Researchers have found that stress and depression kill the neurons in a region called the 'Hippocampus.' The antidepressants hence should be causing the formation of new neurons in this region. Drugs like Prozac, which are selective serotonin reuptake inhibitors, increase the concentration of a protein called BDNF in certain regions of the human brain. BDNF stands for 'Brain-Derived Neurotrophic Factor.' BDNF plays a vital role in producing new neurons in the human brain's hippocampus which leads to feeling of betterment among those suffering from depression. It is for this reason you don't see an immediate improvement in the symptoms among the patients taking the antidepressants.

"Scientists are challenging the theory that the dip in serotonin concentration is solely responsible for depression. Researchers are also interested in knowing if depression like other diseases is linked to the disturbance in the gut microbiome."

Kidnapper: "You mean it is the microbes in the gut that are pulling the plug."

Dr. Parker: "Yes, the real key to unlock the actual cause of depression could be hidden in one's gut and not the brain. I mean the disturbances among the colony of bacteria and other microbes in the human gut could be a significant driver of depression."

Kidnapper: "Wow. It seems that the landlords of the human body are the microbes in the gut—the human microbiome?"

Dr. Parker: "Very likely."

Kidnapper: "The next category of drugs is painkillers. However, before we discuss this new category, let us take our students' polls and know where you stand."

Dr. Parker took a long breath. In his quest to answer these questions, he had lost his sense of time. He had one hour left.

Kidnapper: "Let me share the results directly. It is showing 59%. The students are not happy with your answer this time."

Dr. Parker pressed his head with both of his arms and sat down. I need to answer using my secret methodology every time. Being cautious is backfiring me and could harm Rachit - thoughts started clouding Dr. Parker's mind.

Kidnapper: "Come on Dr. Parker. You cannot play for both sides. It is either your country or your son. Don't play with fire."

The kidnapper had read Dr. Parker's mind.

Dr. Parker: "Yes. I will give my best from here on."

Kidnapper: "Better for you.

"Let us restart with the painkillers."

Dr. Parker: "Sure. Let me start with a quote on Pain from Buddhism.

***"Pain is inevitable, suffering is optional."***

"Painkillers or analgesics help reduce the pain.

You see, pain and fever are fundamental evolutionary mechanisms we need for survival.

"Imagine you are an explorer trying to study the flora and fauna of rainforests in Central or South America. Suddenly, you find an ant crawling on your leg. The very next moment, you start jumping and sit with holding your legs tightly. The reason is that you are bitten by an ant and that too by a 'bullet ant'.

"The bullet ants are known for the most painful bite of any insect in the world. You get a throbbing intense pain that lasts for 24 hours. The effect is so strong that it leads to temporary paralysis. It is almost like a bullet hitting you. The pain produced as a response to the ant sting is a protective mechanism. Pain is hence an alarm triggered when something is not right with our body. Something that needs your attention and must be fixed.

"Fever is an alarm, too. It is triggered as soon as the body senses an 'intruder' or unwanted guest in the body. The unwanted guest could be any pathogen, including bacteria, viruses, protozoa, or anything that does not belong to the body."

Kidnapper: "What's the mechanism? How does the brain know the body temperature must be raised during fever?"

Dr. Parker: "The hypothalamus is the temperature-regulating centre in the brain. It is equivalent to a military commander at the borders responsible for getting the army ready during an attack. He has his informers actively looking for any intruder who has illegally entered the human body's territory."

Kidnapper: "Got it. But I have a question. Who is the informer here?"

Dr. Parker: "The informers here are the molecules called 'prostaglandins.' Special Prostaglandins called 'prostaglandins E2' inform the hypothalamus in the brain about the presence of unwelcome guests that are mostly disease-causing microbes. Hypothalamus - our thermostat detects these prostaglandins and raises the body temperature, resulting in what we experience as fever. The most crucial job of fever is to help the immune system's security guards prepare for the upcoming war with microbial intruders. It is like giving a command to the immune system that 'Boys, we are at war. Be ready'. The rise in the body temperature during fever also makes it difficult for our enemies to make their new copies - I mean the microbes.

"The drugs that help lower fever and pain work via a common mechanism. Both of them block the 'Cyclooxygenase' enzymes. The family of these enzymes is called 'COX' collectively. The enzymes control the production of prostaglandin E2 in the body - the primary messengers of the pain that arises due to tissue damage and inflammation. It should not be difficult to imagine what "COX" blockers or inhibitors would do."

Kidnapper: "Of course not. Once the production of prostaglandin E2 is halted, the communication line towards the hypothalamus breaks. The hypothalamus does not get any signals to elevate the body temperature, and your body temperature returns to normal. The doctors have already started their work with antibiotics and other approaches to help you recover faster. However, I still have a question."

Dr. Parker: "What?"

Kidnapper: "What about the humans who lived way before the invention of the antibiotics? How were they treated during fever and infection? We had no antibiotics in those days, but we had the pathogens."

Dr. Parker: "Let your students search for this answer themselves. Sometimes, the journey to find the answer is far more important than the answer itself."

Kidnapper: "Check your WhatsApp, Dr. Parker. I have sent you the poll already.

"I must cross 75% this time, or I will lose Rachit. I am already running out of time," thought Dr. Parker, biting his nails again."

Dr. Parker: "What? 54% only? How is this even possible? I gave my best this time. I don't think this is a fair result."

Kidnapper: "Well, I cannot help here. These are the exact poll results. Since you have the last 50 minutes, you must show your most creative side, or you will lose Rachit."

Dr. Parker: "Ok. I got it. Ask the next question immediately."

Kidnapper: "Here we go. Tell me something about 'Narcotic analgesics.'"

Dr. Parker: "Narcotic analgesics are painkillers that silence the neurons that carry the message of pain. Unlike painkillers like paracetamol and aspirin, narcotic analgesics work by binding to their receptors in the nerve cells present in the brain and spinal cord. In short, they directly attack the headquarters. They are much more potent in silencing the pain messaging relay than your regular painkillers. Doctors prescribe these medicines under exceptional circumstances related to intense pain felt after surgery, pain related to certain cancers, and labour pain."

Kidnapper: "Could you give us some examples of narcotic analgesics?".

Dr. Parker: "Sure. One of the most widely used narcotic analgesics are opioids. This family of chemicals is found in Opium Poppy seeds and has a thousand-year-old history of being used for pain relief. The oldest record of their usage can be traced to papyrus records of Egypt. The discovery of which molecular locks these opioids exactly open is an interesting story. Before I tell you about the discovery of opioid receptors I must discuss an important concept of chemistry. May I ask you a question?"

Kidnapper: "Yes, sure."

Dr. Parker: "What's the difference between C-12 and C-14?"

Kidnapper: "C-14 is a radioactive isotope of Carbon."

Dr. Parker: "Yes. Isotopes are like identical twins where one is heavier than the other. As Bill Bryson said in his book 'A Short History of Nearly Everything,' "Protons give an atom its identity, electrons its personality." Since the isotopes have the same arrangement of electrons, they have similar chemical properties. And hence, if you replace one of the regular carbon atoms in any molecule with C-14, you could actually trace the movement of the molecule and its biological interaction because of the radiation emitted by decaying C-14. We call this method Radiolabeling. It is one of the most widely used methods in research and medicine to track the movement and behaviour of molecules in biological systems.

"In 1973, graduate student Candace Pert at the pharmacology department of John Hopkins University School of Medicine gave radiolabeled Naloxone to animals and found that the opioid blocker interacted with receptors present in the brain and spinal cord. The presence of the opioid receptors led to the natural conclusion that animals must be producing endogenous morphine-like molecules that bind to these receptors present in the brain and spinal cord. In short animals must have their own pain management system. These natural painkillers that bind to the opioid receptors were later named as 'endorphins' and 'enkephalins'. Apart from helping with pain, the endorphins also encourage and reinforce activities linked to survival."

Dr. Parker: "However, the sale of the opioids is strictly controlled by the governments in most of the places."

Kidnapper: "But why? Why would such effective medicines be regulated?"

Dr. Parker: "These medicines carry a risk of severe addiction. Apart from silencing those neurons involved in sending pain signals, the narcotic analgesics also release showers of dopamine once they bind to the opioid receptors in the midbrain. You don't only feel good as the pain has lessened but also feel euphoric. The patient might consume the drug only for the euphoria, even when the pain is gone. The chances of addiction are extremely high among the patients who consume opioids for the management of their pain.

"A lot of countries control the distribution of narcotic painkillers through strict laws. The distributors and the healthcare professionals maintain strict records which are subject to regular inspections."

Kidnapper: "Cool."

Dr. Parker: "Let me tell you something that's even more interesting.

"Scientists are manipulating scorpion venoms to make strong painkillers. They have also discovered painkiller proteins in the venom of the 'mamba' snakes and they have rightly named them 'mambalgins.'"

Kidnapper: "Wow, only scientists could dare to transform a deadly poison into a life-saving elixir. What would be the advantages of such painkillers over conventional ones?"

Dr. Parker: "Painkillers prepared by manipulating the peptides present in the venom might have fewer side effects than the narcotic painkillers used currently. Researchers in Australia are trying to create similar venom-based painkillers. However, certain issues must be solved before we can give these painkillers directly to the patients."

Kidnapper: "My students have some interesting questions on this topic."

Dr. Parker: "I would love to answer them. Please go ahead."

Kidnapper: "The first question is about the working mechanism of venom."

Dr. Parker: "One of the most common category of venoms are called neurotoxins. These neurotoxins directly interfere with different aspects of communication between two neurons or a neuron and a muscle. One of the most common goals of venom is to immobilize the prey."

Kidnapper: "Interesting. I got it. Once the prey is immobilized through paralysis, it is least likely to resist further and would also get killed easily. This makes a lot of sense for the snakes."

Dr. Parker: "You are right. However, scientists believe that the venom is also used as a potent weapon to deter the powerful predators.

"But before we wrap up this topic of narcotic analgesics, I have something interesting to share."

Kidnapper: "What's that?"

Dr. Parker: "I want to tell you about a family in the Italy."

Kidnapper: "What's with them?"

Dr. Parker: "This family does not feel chronic pain. They have such tolerance to pain that they do not know if they have got a fracture."

Kidnapper: "That's quite strange. A fracture would cause unbearable pain. How could they not notice that?"

Dr. Parker: "Well, the family has shown exceptional tolerance to pain. The cause of their superpower or the curse runs into their genes. Faults in the pain-regulating genes made the family less sensitive to the pain. The family has a syndrome named after them called Marsili syndrome. Individuals with these mutations are less sensitive to extreme heat, capsaicin in chilli peppers, and bone fractures. They can tolerate the most intense physical pain in the world, and that too, without the support of any narcotic painkiller."

Kidnapper: "That was quite interesting. Let's talk about molecules that were one of the greatest medical breakthroughs. These molecules were once considered the last nail in the coffin for bacteria, but the current scenario seems different from what we expected. I mean, let's talk about 'antibiotics.'"

Dr. Parker: "Sure."

Kidnapper: "My students want to understand the working mechanism of antibiotics."

Dr. Parker: "To kill any microbial life form, be it bacteria or virus, you must target the processes that keep them alive. Two things are fundamental to any microbial life on this planet. They all need proteins for survival, and they must make copies of their genetic material as required. A bacterial cell is like a company where work is assigned to different departments. All the departments strive to achieve a common goal - survival and the company's growth. A marketing department handles all the branding efforts while HR hires the best possible talents to fulfil the specific roles.

"Similarly, the different compartments in the cell that we call 'organelles' work in coordination for the survival and reproduction of the cell. There are mitochondria which fuel the entire system by supplying energy. It is rightfully called the 'powerhouse of the cell.' On the other hand, you have ribosomes who carry the most important responsibilities on their shoulder - making proteins that keep the cell alive. A large number of the antibiotics target these protein-making machines. The antibiotics stick to the ribosomes and halt the production of bacterial proteins.

"No life form could survive without making copies of their genetic material. If the cell is the hardware, then the genetic material is the software that runs the system. Once your software is corrupt, it does not matter, even if you have the world's best hardware. Certain antibiotics would interfere with this software installation and turn your hardware into useless trash. I mean, there is a category of antibiotics that interfere with the copying process of the genetic material among the bacteria.

"Have you ever visited any fort in your life? Let's say the Mehrangarh fort or the Kumbhalgarh fort in Rajasthan, India."

Kidnapper: "Not really. I have heard of them."

Dr. Parker: "The kings of these regions made those grand walls around the forts to protect their kingdom. Imagine yourself as a king who has ordered his people to make a similar wall. But whenever your boys do some construction, an enemy stops your workers from doing anything. In such a scenario, building a wall for you would be challenging, and so would be to control who comes inside your kingdom and who goes out. You will get weak and prone to attacks. Your kingdom will die out soon. This is how the third category of antibiotics kills the bacteria. Like an enemy that stops workers from building the defence walls in a kingdom, an antibiotic like penicillin stops the 'transpeptidase' enzyme that constructs the bacterium's cell wall."

Kidnapper: "Interesting analogy. I guess penicillin has a background story. Please share the story with our students."

Dr. Parker: "Sure, I would love to. I love to talk about the history of scientific discoveries. There is so much to learn from the scientists who go into the depths of nature's ocean and bring out the pearls of truth. Like each one of us, they had their motivations, setbacks, failures, and victories. We must share these stories with our students, too.

"Alexander Fleming revolutionized medicine forever through his gift of penicillin to humanity. He was knighted for his work and awarded the Nobel Prize that he shared with Howard Florey and Ernst Chain in 1945. However, you will be surprised that penicillin wasn't his most important work. I am not saying this. Fleming himself had expressed this sentiment. But what could be more dear to Fleming than his Nobel Prize-winning work or the work that made him a household name? The work is related to snot or the nasal mucus that flows from our nose when we suffer from a common cold."

Kidnapper: "What? I cannot believe this. How could work related to snot or nasal discharge be more important than penicillin? We all thought that penicillin would have been Alexander Fleming's favourite work. The discovery of penicillin is undoubtedly among the most critical events in the history of modern medicine. Isn't it?"

Dr. Parker: "I agree. But it is not me but Fleming who considered his work on experiments with nasal discharge his most important work. And soon, you will believe that, too. Let me narrate the entire story first."

Kidnapper: "I am dying to hear that story. Please continue."

Dr. Parker: "Before I discuss this critical work of Fleming, let me unravel what ignited Fleming's desire to search for solutions to cure infections. This was the year 1914, and World War I had started. Fleming was asked to join the Royal Army Medical Corps in Boulogne, France, and serve the British Army in his capacity as a doctor. They had turned a casino into a medical camp. Fleming saw his fellow citizens dying of septic infections linked to the war injuries, and he felt almost helpless about it. Those deaths of the British soldiers deeply moved Fleming, and he wanted to do something about it.

"Back at St. Mary's Hospital, Fleming was often seen to be lost in deep thought. He would try anything and everything as a prospective cure for infections. And this is not an overstatement."

Kidnapper: "What do you mean by everything?"

Dr. Parker: "Fleming was suffering from the common cold, and this time, he thought of checking if his nasal mucus had any antibacterial properties. The idea of designing an experiment to explore the antibacterial properties of nasal mucus was not only creative but bold, too."

Kidnapper: "Why would you call it bold?"

Dr. Parker: "I called it bold because this was the era when the human body was considered incapable of producing anything that could kill bacteria. With his nasal discharge experiment, Fleming directly challenged this long-held belief."

Kidnapper: "I got it. Fleming, too, like any other great scientist, had the childlike curiosity and guts to go against the mighty tides of prevalent dogmas."

Dr. Parker: "Indeed he was. Now, coming to Fleming's experiment. Fleming checked his nasal discharge against certain bacteria cultures he had grown in his lab.

"After some days of putting the nasal mucus blob in a culture dish, Fleming found that the bacteria did not grow near the mucus drop. Fleming commented, "This is interesting," an understatement according to V. Allison, who had worked with Fleming for a long time. Fleming took Allison's help and checked other body fluids for similar antibacterial effects. This time, they set their eyes on tears. Onion was used to make people cry artificially and collect tears via a pipette. However, the onion was insufficient to produce enough tears, so they had to shift to lemons. The lemon peels were quite handy and met the tear quantity requirement when squeezed in front of the eyes. What's interesting in this experiment is that Fleming convinced other lab assistants in the hospital to volunteer. The volunteers were paid 3 pence for their contribution."

Kidnapper: "Did they try any other body fluids?"

Dr. Parker: "Yes, they tried almost everything. This included blood serum, sputum, semen, saliva, and fluid in ovarian cysts. Animal and plant-based materials were tested too.

"Almost every sample they tested had this antibacterial property. The bacteria-killing property in these body

    THE CURIOUS CASE OF DR. PRAGYAN PARKER

fluids boiled down to the 'lysozyme' enzyme. They used the word 'lyse' to show that it could dissolve bacteria into it, i.e., cause their lysis. The word 'zyme' was added to convey that it was an 'enzyme'.

"Lysozyme was capable of killing many bacteria, but it was ineffective against the ones that made us sick. This meant that lysozyme was limited in its usage in treating people for their infections. However, Fleming's work on Lysozyme became monumental in immunology and bacteriology. The world finally learned that the human body does have a stock of molecular weapons to deal with bacterial invasion."

Kidnapper: "Wow. I am impressed. This was an intriguing tale of curiosity, courage, and commitment. But what about penicillin? When did Fleming make this world-changing discovery?"

Dr. Parker: "Great scientists possessed unique qualities that helped them unravel the secrets of nature, from Einstein, who had the superpower to conduct thought experiments in his head, to Charles Darwin, who had exceptional observational skills, diligence, and intellectual courage."

Kidnapper: "What was Fleming's superpower?"

Dr. Parker: "Fleming was untidy. This was his greatest superpower."

Kidnapper: "Untidy? How could that be a superpower?"

Dr. Parker: "Fleming, unlike some other scientists, did not believe in throwing their test tubes and petri dishes once the job was done. Hence, he kept many culture plates lying as they were before he left for his six-week summer vacation in 1928.

"When Fleming returned to his lab, he observed a mould on one of his *Staphylococci* petri dishes. This was not something unique he was looking at. Foreign bodies had registered their presence in Fleming's lab earlier, too. However, what came as a real surprise was the dissolution of pathogenic bacteria like *Staphylococci* around the fungus."

Kidnapper: "I guess Flemings's experience with nasal mucus would have made him instantly realise the antibacterial action of the mould. He had seen something like this during his nasal discharge experiments. The bacterial population being wiped out in a certain region of the petri dish."

Dr. Parker: "Indeed, the experience with the nasal discharge experiment was of great importance here. The next thing that Fleming did was to pick up a piece of the mould with a scalpel and culture it using nutrient media. As Fleming called it, the mould juice was tested against various pathogenic bacteria that caused diseases like Gonorrhoea, Scarlet fever, and strep throat. One of Fleming's colleagues helped him identify the mould as *Penicillium*."

Kidnapper: "What about penicillin? How did Fleming extract the actual missile that was hitting the right targets? The wonder molecule of 'Penicillin.'"

Dr. Parker: "Fleming was a microbiologist and lacked the expertise to extract the active molecule from the mould. It was not until 1939 that Fleming came across people interested in extracting penicillin. The two other stars of the penicillin story are Howard Florey and Fleming's Oxford colleague Ernst Chain. The duo could extract, stabilise, and purify the compound. The wonder molecule was tested on animals and found to be safe. Safety is one of the most important properties you would expect from a potential medicine to be used in humans."

Kidnapper: "When did we first succeed using penicillin? I mean, who was the first patient to survive after taking penicillin?"

Dr. Parker: "Let me give you some context before we discuss the first case.

"Even today, when we have modern medicine at its peak, more than 150,000 women and infants die of Group B *Streptococcus* infection. Imagine what would have happened if the world had not heard of antibiotics.

"A 33-year-old lady survived her strep infection that she had got post-miscarriage. Not only did the lady recover from her fever, but she also went up to live for 60 more years. This was the first-ever case where penicillin saved a precious human life from a life-threatening infection."

Kidnapper: "But the scenario has changed these days. The bacteria laugh at our molecular weapons, which we were once so proud of. These pathogens can proudly swim in fluids laden with antibiotics and remain unaffected. Antibiotic resistance is widespread and a global health concern. Our students would like to know about multiple drug-resistant bacteria or 'Superbugs.'"

Dr. Parker: "The superbugs have properties that most bacteria do not have. They can be compared to "Hulk,"

Iron Man," and my favourite "Spider-Man" as even the most powerful molecular weapons invented by humans are useless in front of them. This qualifies as a superpower as far as bacteria are concerned. Alexander Fleming warned that aggressive and irrational use of penicillin or any antibiotic could favour the evolution of antibiotic-resistant bacteria."

Kidnapper: "What are we doing about this problem?"

Dr. Parker: "We have badly failed in terms of using chemicals to control or kill the kind of life we do not want. This includes the herbicides used to kill unwanted plants and the pesticides sprinkled to eliminate the pests that harm the crops. In all these cases, life has found a way to escape. The newly evolved version of the plant or pest can easily tolerate the chemicals that killed them earlier. In a short period, a new variety emerges and makes a fool out of humans.

"The same is the case with antibiotics. It is all about the irrational, selfish, and excessive use of chemicals here. Unless and until we see every organism as a part of the biosphere where we are a co-habitant and not a dictator, the world will not become a better place. The bacteria can evolve so fast that they always find a way to get ahead of us. A new antibiotic launched today might not work in the next 2 years. Antibiotic manufacturing has become less lucrative for pharmaceutical companies as developing a novel molecule takes years and billions of dollars. The company wants to sell the antibiotic for a sufficient time to get a sound return on investment. However, the tiny bacteria don't care about the pharma business. They evolve resistance and render the molecule useless."

Kidnapper: "That's sad. What are the researchers at the universities doing about it? Or anyone else, for that matter?"

Dr. Parker: "They are trying a couple of exciting things. One of them is using viruses to kill bacteria."

Kidnapper: "Viruses? Why would viruses kill bacteria?"

Dr. Parker: "We have been using viruses as microbial assassins for quite some time. The time has ripened to move them from the labs to the clinics. Soon, you might be given solutions containing bacteriophages instead of bitter-tasting antibiotic tablets and capsules against bacterial infections.

"Viruses, as you might have heard, need a foreign cell to complete their life cycle. They need to have the right tools necessary to make their copies. They, therefore, prefer to hijack the cell-copying machinery of a cell belonging to a different life form. From the mighty tigers to tiny bacteria, viruses infect everyone. The cells they infect to make their copies are called host cells, and the viruses that use bacterial cells as their host go by the name 'bacteriophages'.

"As per an estimate, there are some $10^{32}$ bacteriophage particles on Earth. The bacteriophages follow two different lifestyles for their survival and reproduction. The one that kills the bacteria is the 'lytic' cycle, which is preferred when there is no shortage of bacteria hosts. The less aggressive or the 'lysogenic' cycle is preferred when there is a shortage of the bacterial host. Aggressive killing could make the virus extinct as it may run out of hosts to continue its life cycle. Viruses take their chances wisely.

"During the lytic cycle, viruses hijack the cell-copying machinery of the host cell after entering it. Once the virus hijacks the bacterial cell machinery, it halts the production of host proteins and redirects it to synthesize its own proteins. The proteins and viral genetic material produced in the bacterial cell are assembled to form new baby viruses. The bacterial cell bursts, and the virus particles come out. These mature virus particles infect other bacteria hosts to continue their life cycle. Since the cell is lysed at the end of this cycle, it is rightly called the 'lytic cycle' of the bacteriophages.

"What's interesting about bacteriophages is that they infect almost every bacterium on this planet. More importantly, they are specific. Unlike antibiotics, which would also kill friendly bacteria in the body, bacteriophages would kill a specific species. That's a major advantage over antibiotics, which cannot differentiate between a friend and an enemy.

"We recently saw a breakthrough in the treatment of multiple drug-resistant infections using bacteriophages. Researchers from Yale used bacteriophages to successfully treat a patient with a heart infection."

Kidnapper: "Wow. The bacteriophages seem to be a promising alternative to antibiotics."

Dr. Parker: "I agree. The bacteriophage could be used to treat regular infections in the future. However, it has its issues. First, we will need more evidence among human patients regarding the effectiveness of bacteriophages against different pathogenic bacteria. As it happens with antibiotics, the bacteria could also evolve resistance against the bacteriophages. Through future experiments,

     THE CURIOUS CASE OF DR. PRAGYAN PARKER

we will make those black clouds of doubts wither and the ray of hope shine."

Kidnapper: "Let's hope so. What else do the scientists have in their arsenal? Is there a new weapon in the making?"

Dr. Parker: "You must have heard of Cholera."

Kidnapper: "Of course I do."

Dr. Parker: "Cholera is a disease caused by the bacteria *Vibrio cholerae*. Diarrhoea is a classic symptom of cholera, and the bacteria secretes a special toxin to make their human host go to the washroom so frequently. Do you know that before the bacteria release toxins to attack the cells in the intestine, they communicate with fellow bacteria and plan their attack? Do you know they have a social network?"

Kidnapper: "Here we go. I am sure you are again taking this too far. How could bacteria plan things?"

Dr. Parker: "Ok. I agree that the bacteria cannot plan an attack. However, they talk to other bacteria before releasing a toxin to attack the host."

Kidnapper: "And may I please know how that communication happens?"

Dr. Parker: "Natural selection has helped bacteria develop their chemical language, expressed through releasing certain molecules and coordinating activities like the production of toxins. These chemical codes called 'autoinducers' are released by bacteria in the surrounding area and taken up by neighbouring ones. Once the bacteria sense a critical concentration of these autoinducers around them, they release the toxin together, making the attack against the host more effective. Researchers have observed this chemical communication among the bacteria of the species *Vibrio fischeri and Vibrio cholerae*. 'Quorum sensing' is the word scientists use to describe this social communication of the bacteria."

Kidnapper: "Interesting."

Dr. Parker: "Researchers have found that bacteria use quorum sensing in biofilm formation."

Kidnapper: "Biofilm. What's that? Don't tell me that bacteria also make cinema."

Dr. Parker: "Not really. A biofilm is like a bacterial city where all the cells stick together on a surface. The biofilms play a major role in helping the bacteria fight antibiotics effectively. Scientists across the world are trying to understand how these bacterial cities are built so that they can prevent their formation or destroy the existing ones. The biofilm disruption could be our next masterstroke in dealing with life-threatening bacterial infections. It all boils down to stopping quorum sensing or molecular communication among the bacteria."

Kidnapper: "Can bacteria from one species sense chemical codes produced by bacteria from a different species? Is there any bacterial spy agency or BI-6?"

Dr. Parker: "BI-6?"

Kidnapper: "I mean 'Bacterial Intelligence-6'."

Dr. Parker: "Haha. I am not sure. However, recent experiments have shown that certain bacterial species can indeed listen to the code released by another species."

*Professor Alexander Fleming, holder of the Chair of Bacteriology at London University, who first discovered the mould Penicillin notatum. Here in his laboratory at St Mary's, Paddington, London (1943).*

Kidnapper: "Thank you so much for all that knowledge. Can you tell us something about the classification of antibiotics?"

Dr. Parker: "Sure. Antibiotics are broadly classified into two categories. Bacteriostatic antibiotics, which stop the growth of bacteria, include molecules like chloramphenicol, tetracycline, and erythromycin. Bactericidal antibiotics, on the other hand, are merciless in killing bacteria. Bactericidal antibiotics comprise Aminoglycosides, Ofloxacin, and Fluoroquinolones.

"Antibiotics that kill both gram-positive and gram-negative bacteria are called broad-spectrum antibiotics. This is obvious because they kill a broad class of bacteria. The antibiotics that are choosy in terms of whom they would kill are called 'narrow-spectrum' antibiotics. The last category of antibiotics kills a particular species of bacteria and is called a 'limited spectrum' antibiotic."

Kidnapper: "It's time for the results, Dr. Parker. I guess you have some last 30 minutes. Shall I send the results?"

Dr. Parker: "Of course. This is my last chance to save Rachit. If I do not get a favourable response, I will lose my son."

Kidnapper: "Here you go, Dr. Parker. Check your WhatsApp."

Dr. Parker was sweating profusely. He was afraid as no WhatsApp notification was ever more important than this one. Drops of sweat fell on his screen as he brought the phone closer to unlock it. He pressed 1307 on the number lock and saw a new WhatsApp notification. He opened WhatsApp to see a poll percentage of 95%.

Dr. Parker took a deep breath, and with the exhalation, his tension was released, too. Drops of water fell again on the phone screen, but this time, they were tears.

Kidnapper: "Congratulations, Dr. Parker. This is the highest percentage you have achieved so far. Great job. Now, take 2000 steps straight and 500 steps on the right, and you will see a cottage with a red light."

Dr. Parker took those steps possibly faster than Usain Bolt. He could see that red light. The ray of hope came with those particles of red photon as Dr. Parker watched the red light eagerly. This red light had a dual nature - it made him anxious as he was running out of time and hopeful as he was close to this end goal.

Kidnapper: "You have finally reached the last stage. I know that you are close. But a negative review of your next answer would destroy every one of your efforts so far. Be cautious and try to be as engaging as possible."

Dr. Parker: "Of course. I am ready."

Kidnapper: "The next category of drugs is anti-fertility drugs. Would you shed some light on them, Dr. Parker? And remember, you are also running out of time. You have 30 minutes to save Rachit."

Dr. Parker: "Anti-fertility drugs are used to prevent pregnancy. Some of these drugs suppress the production of eggs in females and also make their union with sperm difficult. The drugs manage this feat by increasing the thickness of mucus in the cervix. It is like you want to prevent an expert swimmer from reaching the other end of the swimming pool by making the water as thick as honey. The other mechanism through which these drugs prevent pregnancy is that they slow down the movement of eggs through the fallopian tubes. As the name suggests, fallopian tubes are tube-like structures that connect the ovaries with the uterus. The anti-fertility drugs also prevent the implantation of the fertilised egg in the uterus.

"These drugs contain a mixture of derivatives of female sex hormones like synthetic oestrogen and progesterone."

Kidnapper: "Are we the only species that can control the birth of their progenies?"

Dr. Parker: "Have you heard of 'embryonic diapause'?"

Kidnapper: "No."

Dr. Parker: "'Embryonic diapause' is an evolved reproductive strategy to help species give birth only when the conditions outside are favourable for the survival of mother and the upcoming progeny. In embryonic diapause, the embryo is frozen at an early stage. The entire effort and energy invested in nourishing the embryo will be wasted if the chances of survival outside are meagre. The survival challenges could come from factors like lack of food resources or poor weather conditions. 'Embryonic diapause' has been recorded in some 130 species of mammals so far. Marsupials like Kangaroo and Roe deer are widely known to undergo embryonic diapause. Stopping the embryo's growth is involuntary, and the animal has no conscious control over it."

Kidnapper: "Hmmm...when does the embryo move on from the blastocyst stage? I mean, what's the usual length of this dormancy in case of the embryonic diapause?"

Dr. Parker: "This could take months. By the way, have you heard of Kanupriya Agarwal? She was born in 1978 in India."

Kidnapper: "So what? There must have been so many Indians born in 1978. What's so special about Kanupriya?"

Dr. Parker: "Kanupriya Agarwal is a testimony of India's capability to achieve scientific breakthroughs while we were still a young democracy. In a country that lacked fundamental research facilities, an Indian physician managed to produce the world's second test-tube baby.

"Yes, Kanupriya Agarwal was India's first and the world's second test-tube baby born after 67 days of Louise Brown, the world's first test-tube baby. This was a monumental achievement for a country like India. More importantly, the Indian method of producing test-tube babies or in-vitro fertilization was better than that of its British counterparts. Today the method pioneered by Indian scientist is the most widely employed method for in-vitro fertilisation."

Kidnapper: "And may I know who invented this method?"

Dr. Parker: "The genius behind this discovery helped thousands become moms and dads when they gave up their hope. Holding your son or daughter for the first time is the most beautiful feeling in the world. I can still remember holding Rachit vividly. My life changed after that day. I became more responsible and the started on a journey to become the best version of myself. So many men and women worldwide would agree that parenting provides one of the most significant opportunities to grow in life.

"Anyway, let me come to the man behind India's first test-tube baby. How many of us know his name? It's high time to celebrate unsung heroes like Dr. Subhas Mukherjee."

Kidnapper: "Oh... So it is Dr. Subhas Mukherjee."

Dr. Parker: "The genius doctor we are celebrating here is Dr. Subhas Mukherjee. Dr. Subhas Mukherjee was born in 1931 in Hazaribagh, a district in Jharkhand. He studied at the National Medical College in Kolkata and showed a strong interest in research, even as a medical student. Dr. Mukherjee completed his PhD in Reproductive Physiology at the University of Calcutta.

"Dr. Subhas also obtained his second PhD in reproductive endocrinology from the University of Edinburgh, UK. Endocrinology is the study of hormones, and Dr. Mukherjee was interested in the hormones associated with the human reproductive system.

"Soon after returning to India, Dr. Mukherjee started his research on the formation of human sperm and egg. Others shared his passion for research, too. One of them was Dr. Sunit Mukherjee, who was a "cryobiologist." A "Cryobiologist" is interested in understanding ultra-low temperatures' role on living organisms or biological systems. The second person who assisted Dr. Mukherjee in his pioneering IVF work was Dr. Saroj Kanti Bhattacharya, a gynaecologist."

Kidnapper: "Could you briefly explain the process of in-vitro fertilisation?"

Dr. Parker: "The word "in vivo" is used for processes taking place inside a living organism, whereas "in-vitro" is attributed to those done outside the body in a laboratory. So IVF or "In-vitro fertilisation" refers to the successful meeting of egg and sperm in a petri dish outside the female body. IVF treatment is preferred when the conditions in the female body do not support different aspects of fertilisation and pregnancy. Severe low sperm count among the male members is also one of the primary reasons that couples choose IVF.

"Now the first step of IVF is to get an egg from the lady. This is where the British scientists who pioneered IVF and Dr. Subhas Mukherjee used different roads to reach the same destination. British scientists waited for the natural release of the egg while Dr. Mukherjee induced the ovaries to release the egg when required by giving the female hormone 'Gonadotropin.' Nowadays, modern clinics globally use Dr. Mukherjee's approach of stimulating the ovaries to produce multiple eggs."

Kidnapper: "How are the eggs collected?"

Dr. Parker: "The eggs are collected through a minor surgical procedure. This involves collecting the eggs using a thin needle guided to reach the ovaries via ultrasound.

"The next stage is to collect the sperm from the male donor. Post collection, the egg and sperm are made to mingle together successfully in the laboratory. In some instances, doctors may directly inject a sperm into an egg via a process called "Intracytoplasmic Sperm Injection" or ICSI. The fertilised eggs are monitored and kept in a particular lab environment so that they can develop into early-stage embryos. The embryos are transferred to the woman's uterus in the next stage. The doctors would then perform tests about 2 weeks after the embryo transfer. This is required to confirm pregnancy.

"Dr. Subhas Mukherjee used this procedure to help Bela Agarwal get successfully pregnant. The procedure became one of the most significant scientific experiments in the history of mankind. On October 3, 1978, Bela Agarwal gave birth to Durga during the auspicious Durga Puja - a festival which celebrates feminine energy and divinity. Durga Agarwal, a girl child, became a testament to India's scientific capabilities that could accomplish lofty goals even in resource-poor settings. Durga was the world's second test-tube baby, born after 67 days of Louise Brown, the world's first test-tube baby. English scientists RG Edwards and Patrick Steptoe received massive attention and wider acclaim for their work on in-vitro fertilisation in the UK. At the same time, here in India, Dr. Mukherjee was ignored and humiliated.

"This was the India of the 70s. There was a serious stigma attached to a woman who was childless. Bela Agarwal knew what holding Durga in her hands meant to her. However, irrespective of her gratitude for Dr. Subhas, she had to keep this a secret. The family wanted to avoid every possible media attention. Unfortunately, this also meant that Dr. Subhas Mukherjee could not publicly talk about Durga or present her. Things did not get better for Dr. Subhas anytime soon. The medical and scientific community sidelined Dr. Mukherjee instead of celebrating his contributions. The state government followed in the same footsteps after an expert panel rejected Dr. Mukherjee's work. I don't know how the panel failed to see a miracle that manifested in their own country. The central government banned Dr. Mukherjee from discussing and sharing his work on international forums."

Kidnapper: "I don't have words to describe Dr. Mukherjee's pain."

Dr. Parker: "Dr. Subhas Mukherjee could not take this humiliation any longer. On June 19, 1981, Dr. Mukherjee committed suicide. He left a note that said, "I can't wait every day for a heart attack to kill me." With the death of Dr. Subhas Mukherjee, India not only lost a scientist but also a hero who could have inspired Indians to believe in their scientific abilities and dreams. A decade later, celebrated and national award-winning Indian director, Tapan Sinha, made a film partly inspired by the life of Dr. Subhas Mukherjee.

"Although belated, the Indian medical community acknowledged Dr. Mukherjee's contributions in October 2003. The Indian Council of Medical Research organised a function on the 25th anniversary of Kanupriya Agarwal, also known as Durga. "I am not a trophy but proud to be the living example of the work of a genius. Justice has been done to my scientific dad," said Kanupriya during the event. The entire credit for bringing the story of Dr. Mukherjee to the world goes to Dr. TC Anand Kumar.

"Dr. TC Anand Kumar is credited for India's first IVF-assisted birth, documented in a scientific journal. He thought of himself as the first Indian to have done IVF, as he was unaware of Dr. Mukherjee's work. During a scientific conference, he met Dr. Sunit Mukherjee, one of Dr. Mukherjee's team members. Sunit Mukherjee informed Dr. TC Anand Kumar about the pioneering work of Dr. Subhas Mukherjee and also handed him the original notes. After studying those notes, Dr. TC Anand Kumar was convinced of Dr. Subhas Mukherjee's work and felt a compulsion to tell his story to the world. He published an article on the scientific achievements of Dr. Subhas Mukherjee in the journal "Current Science" in 1997 and made the world aware of an unsung genius."

Kidnapper: "That's so nice of him. When did the folks abroad invent the technique that Dr. Mukherjee used?"

Dr. Parker: "Dr. Subhas Mukherjee had successfully stored the eight-cell embryo under low-temperature conditions for 53 days. The Western world took 5 years to achieve the same feat. Dr. Subhas Mukherjee was far ahead of his time. I think his death was a loss to the whole world.

"While the world is slowly recognising the genius of Dr. Subhas Mukherjee, Dr. Robert Edwards won the 2010 Nobel Prize in Physiology and Medicine for his work on in-vitro fertilisation."

Kidnapper: "There was so much to learn from this story, Dr. Parker. It was heart-touching and wrenching at the same time. Is there something you would like to tell the students apart from academics? But check your watch first."

Dr. Parker: "Oh my God. It is showing the last 10 minutes."

Kidnapper: "These are the most important 10 minutes of your life. Go ahead and give your best."

Dr. Parker: "I would insist that the students learn from my stories I am going to share now. I have discussed science so far; now, I want to talk about the most important things often neglected in the classroom or conventional school setup."

Kidnapper: "Is it a new subject or something?"

Dr. Parker: "I will share stories about the most crucial subject called 'life'."

Kidnapper: "That's deep. Please go ahead."

Dr. Parker: "This is a story of a boy who was passionate about football from an early age.

"He was born in Spain and wanted to play for Real Madrid and his national football team. The boy worked hard on his game from age 10 and became great at goalkeeping.

"At 18, he had reached a stage where his childhood dream of playing for his favourite club and country was soon to be realised. However, there is no way we could ever think of how life would turn out.

"We never know what obstacles are lying ahead on this road to life. Any tragedy in the future might permanently shatter the castle of our dreams."

Kidnapper: "Are you suggesting the kid was not selected for Real Madrid? You said he had gotten great at the game. What happened then?"

Dr. Parker: "Yes, he was not selected. Because he met with an accident that left him paralysed and bedridden for 2 years."

Kidnapper: "What?"

Dr. Parker: "Yes, On an unfortunate day he and his friends had gone to a party and their car met with a terrible accident in the year 1963. His spine was smashed during this accident, and it was his soul that suffered the most intense damage."

Kidnapper: "Soul? What do you mean by that?"

Dr. Parker: "The consulting doctor was not quite optimistic about Julio's ability to walk. However, they were sure that he would never be able to play football again.

"Life kicked him so hard that his dreams got into a million pieces. He had no idea if he would ever be able to re-assemble himself."

Kidnapper: "Indeed, the most painful sound in the world is when your dreams break down into pieces. Only you would hear that sound, something that would pierce you billions of times like the deadly sting of a scorpion."

Dr. Parker: "Exactly. Imagine what Julio would have gone through.

"His dreams of playing football were no longer a possibility. The news that he would not be able to play football ever changed him completely.

"The road to recovery was not smooth for him. However, something interesting happened later."

Kidnapper: "Did he recover and start playing football again?"

Dr. Parker: "Nope. He managed to do magic, but this time, he used his hand instead of his legs. But before I share the story, I would like you to know what Julio has achieved in life.

"Julio Iglesias is now considered one of history's most successful Latin singers. He has also sold over 100 million records worldwide in 14 languages. Julio has performed in more than 5000 concerts in front of 60 million people from 5 continents. He has won a Grammy and many other notable awards in the music industry. This certainly makes him one of the most significant international singers of all time in every sense."

*Julio Iglesias at the Eurovision Song Contest 1970.*

Kidnapper: "What? How did that happen?"

Dr. Parker: "Well, this development was neither easy nor swift. Julio had a long recovery phase after that tragic accident. He was bedridden for almost 18 months. However, during this period, he started writing poems and songs. It was Eladio Magdaleno who changed Julio's life forever."

Kidnapper: "Who is she? His wife?"

Dr. Parker: "Julio's nurse, Eladio Magdaleno, gave him a guitar to help him recover his hands faster. Julio had never tried the guitar before. However, this was a different time, and with this new instrument came a new realisation. Julio discovered his musical talent. He learned that apart from football, something else enchanted his soul.

"In 1968, after coming out of almost 5 years of hospitalisation, Julio wrote a song about his life and won the Benidorm International Song Festival, which was organised in Spain. He ended up signing a deal with Discos Columbia. His first album, Yo Canto, or I Sing, spent 15 weeks on the Spanish charts and peaked at No. 3. The rest, as you know, is history.

"What lessons could students derive from the life of Julio?"

Kidnapper: "When life seems like a black hole, sucking all the dreams you ever had into its eternal darkness, remember that the light of hope will still manage to reach you. The event horizon of the problems cannot trap the light of hope. It is essential to be optimistic and look for that silver lining."

Dr. Parker: "Indeed. Hope is everything in life. It is important to remember that life has no obligation to work according to your plans. The only thing you can do is accept what life offers you and make the best out of it. Trusting the supreme powers with a better plan for us is important. We might be thinking of the moon while the almighty has a plan to help us reach the stars. Just accept what happens and give your best. You should concentrate only on things that are within your control. Put the best of your efforts into every work you do and never worry about the results. Let me share some lines by Anna Sewell that perfectly capture the essence of this idea,

> **"Do your best, And leave the rest, 'Twill all come right Some day or night'."**

Kidnapper: "These are beautiful lines that rightly capture Julio's life's essence. Why don't we train students for the actual exam called life? An exam where failure is a natural part of the journey, and the measure of your success is your ability to rise again after you fall. Your tenacity and persistence are actual areas where you need to score high. Why don't we train our students to fall in love with the journey rather than fantasising about the destination?"

Dr. Parker: "Indeed. When it comes to our students and kids, the real exams we should be worried about are the exams taken by life. This is an exam where the ultimate result is given in terms of how happy you are. And like any other exams, these, too, requires mentorship.

"Let me share another inspiring story here."

Kidnapper: "Dr. Parker, I guess we have 3 minutes left for you. Make sure this last story takes you closer to your goal. Be careful."

Dr. Parker: "This is the story of a boy in Kerala whose parents wanted him to be a doctor.

"Becoming a doctor has been almost like a national dream career in India for a long time and is still an obsession in many small towns. The parents of Senapathy also expected him to become a medical practitioner. They did not have any doctors, not even in the extended family.

"Senapathy was good in his studies and committed to his dream. However, as he entered junior college, he lost the focus required to get into the medical college. Something terrible happened."

Kidnapper: "What?"

Dr. Parker: "Senapathy could not make it to M.B.B.S by a meagre margin of 2 marks."

Kidnapper: "OMG…he must have been devastated, and so would have been his parents."

Dr. Parker: "Indeed, Senapathy was devastated."

Kidnapper: "What happened next? Did he try for M.B.B.S for the next year?"

Dr. Parker: "No, he instead went ahead with the subject he loved. He started his B.Sc in Physics."

Kidnapper: "How did he handle maths in that case?"

Dr. Parker: "He took tuition for maths, and this teacher changed his life completely. He got back the most precious thing Senapathy had lost recently."

Kidnapper: "Let me guess. The maths teacher helped Senapathy regain his 'confidence.'"

Dr. Parker: "Yes. That's what great teachers do. The teacher helped him regain his confidence.

"Senapathy decided to pursue an M.Sc in Physics at IIT Madras and later pursued an M.Tech in computer sciences from the same institute. Senapathy joined Patni Computers as his first company."

Kidnapper: "What is Senapathy doing these days?"

Dr. Parker: "Senapathy's full name is 'Senapathy Gopalakrishnan.' His net worth is more than 1 billion dollars, and his company is valued at around 50 billion dollars.

"It is not about money.

"Senapathy Gopalakrishnan is Mr. Kris Gopalkrishnan, one of the co-founders of Infosys.

"Krish Gopalkrishnan is widely known for his philanthropic activities. He contributed rupees 225 crore to the development of the 'Centre for Brain Research' at the Indian Institute of Science, Bengaluru. He also supports the development of neurocomputing and data science at IISc Bengaluru and IIT Madras.

"Kris is supporting Indian researchers working in the areas of ageing and neurobiology. He is deeply involved with the projects dealing in the history of science in India. His Gopalakrishnan - Deshpande Centre for Innovation and Entrepreneurship at IIT Madras was started to help Indian researchers solve the problems of Indian society using innovation in science and technology."

Kidnapper: "Wow, man. A student who missed his M.B.B.S degree by 2 marks ended up creating a billion-dollar company and contributing to society's welfare by supporting young scientists and institutions.

"My students would never have gotten a lesson like this. These lessons could become the guiding principles for their whole life. Irrespective of what field they choose, they would surely succeed if they followed these principles."

Dr. Parker checked his watch and took a deep breath. He had 10 seconds left.

Dr. Parker: "Can you please share the poll results? I cannot wait anymore to reach Rachit."

Kidnapper: "Check your WhatsApp for the poll results."

Dr. Parker had never waited for any result with such eagerness in his life—not even the result of his PhD selection email from his favourite university. He started jumping like a kid who won a school competition as he read the message, "The satisfaction rate is 100%." Congratulations, Dr. Parker. You did a fantastic job. Take 100 steps to your right, and you will find 3 cottages. Rachit is in the third one.

Dr. Parker ran towards the cottage immediately. The moment he entered the cottage, he saw Rachit wearing his favourite Pokémon Go T-shirt, with a pizza box next to him. His mouth was sealed with black tape, and he was lying unconscious.

Dr. Parker sprinkled some water on his face and shook him up by his shoulders. Rachit opened his eyes and looked at Dr. Parker with drowsy eyes.

"Thank god you are fine," said Dr. Parker, while kissing Rachit's forehead.

"Papa, I want to go home," said Rachit, hugging his dad.

"Sure beta, we are going straight home," said Dr. Parker, holding Rachit's hand.

Kidnapper: "Hello, Dr. Parker. It is time for you to share your secret learning methodology with us. I hope you don't mind. We will not let you go until and unless you teach us your secret learning method."

Dr. Parker: "Well, to be frank, Mr. Kidnapper, my methodology is an open secret."

Kidnapper: "An open secret? What does that even mean?"

Dr. Parker: "Yes. The learning method we planned to implement was always known to the world. Ask your students why they enjoyed my lessons so much? What intrigued them most? I am sure it would be a seven-letter word."

Kidnapper: "Oh... let me check that.

"Hello students, I am sure you enjoyed the session with Dr. Parker. I wanted to know what you liked best about the content," the kidnapper typed and sent the message to the group.

"The best part was the stories," answered a student.

"I liked the personal stories of scientists associated with the discoveries and inventions," said another student.

The most common reason the students loved the content was the stories.

Kidnapper: "Yes, Dr. Parker, now I got your point. The answer is a seven-letter word - 'stories'. Even for me, the best part of your answers was those stories."

Dr. Parker: "Yup. The best way we remember any information is through stories. Our ancestors always knew this fact about learning. For this reason, the most important lessons related to morality, ethics, health, safety, relationships, and others have always been shared in the form of stories.

"To my surprise, our ancient teachers better understood human learning than we do. They knew that the human brain is a story-processing device, and stories are its favourite format for storing information. The fruit of knowledge, when wrapped up in a narrative, becomes tastier and easier to digest. Lessons taught in the form of stories go deep down memory lane and are accessible in the blink of a thought."

Kidnapper: "Oh yes. For the same reason, the wisdom required to live a good life has been shared in the form of stories across all cultures in the world. Storytelling is deeply rooted in the human psyche—be it ancient scriptures, dances, or paintings - we see storytelling everywhere.

"Oh my goodness. How can I miss this? Storytelling is the greatest superpower humans uniquely possess. And yes, our ancestors have always known the importance of storytelling in spreading knowledge that they felt was important for us to thrive."

Dr. Parker: "Indeed. However, creating content where scientific concepts are interwoven within stories is an entirely different game. Designing a curriculum that engages students while ensuring they learn the subject proficiently requires an expert like me. And since I have Rachit back, I don't think I shall help you further. I have no intention of sharing my work except with agencies that work for my country, directly or indirectly."

Kidnapper: "Our entire team knows how patriotic you are. Each of the students hiding here knows you. But I am sure you would change your mind once I reveal my intentions."

Dr. Parker: "I am not sure."

Kidnapper: "Let me tell you something. Myself and every student who has listened to you so far are refugees.

A year ago, we were an ethnic minority few people knew about. The current government wanted to wipe us out completely. However, we escaped and now we are trying to lay a strong foundation for our people and the future generation by creating a new nation. We want them to have all the opportunities they might need to grow and become responsible citizens. The most important thing we want to teach them is empathy and care for the world around them, including every non-human life. We want them to realise that this pale blue dot, known as Earth, is the only planet we know that has life so far. As humans, being the most intelligent and powerful species, we must also be the most responsible. Like every other species, we are lucky to have this home, which belongs to us equally. Hence, it's essential to live in harmony, not only with fellow humans but with other species too. If we fail to appreciate life around us, we will be wiped out completely. What happened during COVID-19 was just a teaser. Imagine how dangerous the entire film could be. We need your support, Dr. Parker, to build solid foundations and implant these ideas deeply in our students' minds. Only through the right education can we inculcate the right values among students. This will lead to a more peaceful world as education leaders across the globe use your work to educate and ignite young minds. It would lead to a more peaceful world and be in everyone's interest, including your country's.

"Imagine if Watson and Crick had refused to share their work with the world. Would we have developed the technology that has been saving millions of people globally by directly influencing healthcare and agriculture? What if Jonas Salk had denied other countries the use of his polio vaccines?"

These arguments deeply impacted Dr. Parker and took him back in time. He remembered how generous and supportive his mentors from abroad were, who helped him become a leader in science. They never let their nationalities interfere with the student-teacher relationship. Dr. Parker had witnessed the selflessness of a teacher-student relationship that transcends national, religious, caste, and other artificial boundaries created by humans. He had been a significant beneficiary of such relationships. How could he deny genuine students the opportunity to learn something just because they weren't born in his country? This was against the educational ideology and teachings of his favourite teachers, whom he admired most.

Dr. Parker: "I had lost my way. I agree with everything you've said. A better education system that teaches kids empathy and kindness and helps them build strong character would benefit everyone, including my country, in the long run. As someone mentored by foreign teachers, I cannot deny others that opportunity. How could I oppose the tradition that helped me become the scientist and educator I am today? By doing so, I would be disrespecting my teachers - my heroes. Although I don't think kidnapping my son was the right way to get me on board, I understand your intentions and will guide you. It's time to practice 'Vasudhaiva Kutumbakam.'"

Kidnapper: "I am sorry for that. We never intended to harm your family. We just wanted your attention and, hopefully, to change your mind about supporting us. Nothing else."

Dr. Parker: "Now I understand."

Kidnapper: "Thank you so much, Dr. Parker. Thank you very much."

"It has gotten late. I guess we shall go home, Rachit," said Dr. Parker while holding Rachit's hand tightly.

# Notes and References

## Impact of Artificial Lights on Glow-Worms

Moubarak EM, David Fernandes AS, Stewart AJA, Niven JE. "Artificial light impairs local attraction to females in male glow-worms." J Exp Biol. 2023 Jun 1;226(11):jeb245760. DOI: 10.1242/jeb.245760. Epub 2023 Jun 13. PMID: 37311409; PMCID: PMC10281516. Accessed at https://www.smithsonianmag.com/science-nature/the-whispering-trees-180968084/.

## Suzanne Simard's Work on Tree Communication

Smithsonian Magazine Article: This article discusses Suzanne Simard's research on tree communication and the division in the scientific community regarding the perception of trees as superorganisms. Accessed at: Smithsonian Magazine. "The Whispering Trees." https://www.smithsonianmag.com/science-nature/the-whispering-trees-180968084/.

TED Talk: Suzanne Simard discusses her research on how trees communicate using a fungal network. Available at: TED. "How Trees Talk to Each Other." https://www.ted.com/talks/suzanne_simard_how_trees_talk_to_each_other?language=en.

## Giraffe and Acacia Co-evolution

Book Reference: "The Hidden Life of Trees" by Peter Wohlleben. The author discusses the different senses among the plants and their communication mechanism, including the story of the Giraffe and Acacia co-evolution. Wohlleben, P. (2016). The Hidden Life of Trees: What They Feel, How They Communicate - Discoveries from a Secret World. Greystone Books.

**National Geographic Article:** Discusses how the acacia plant tries to make the ant dependent on it. https://www.nationalgeographic.com/animals/article/131106-ants-tree-acacia-food-mutualism

**Cardiovascular Adaptations in Giraffes:** This article deals with the different cardiovascular adaptations among giraffes against chronic high blood pressure. Natterson-Horowitz B, et al. Did giraffe cardiovascular evolution solve the problem of heart failure with preserved ejection fraction? Evol Med Public Health. 2021 Jun 11;9(1):248-255. doi: 10.1093/emph/eoab016. PMID: 34447575; PMCID: PMC838.

**Kudu and Acacia Leaves:** Animals like kudus could die from higher doses of acacia leaves. Moore PA. The hidden power of smell: how chemicals influence our lives and behavior. Springer, New York, 2016.

**Symbiotic Relationship Between Acacia and Ants:** Moore PA. The hidden power of smell: how chemicals influence our lives and behavior. Springer, New York, 2016.

## Co-evolution of Tomato Plants and Caterpillars

Article on the arms race between tomato plants and caterpillars. Accessed at: Penn State News. "Silencing the Alarm." https://www.psu.edu/news/research/story/silencing-alarm/.

## Japanese Scientists Capture Plant Communication in Real-Time

A team of Japanese scientists captured real-time footage of plants communicating through airborne compounds released under stress. Accessed at: https://www.sciencelink.net/features/plant-communication-visualised/21600.article.

## Pollination Strategy of Rafflesia Flower

Article on the pollination strategy of the Rafflesia flower. Accessed at: Harvard Magazine. "Colossal Blossom." https://www.harvardmagazine.com/2017/02/colossal-blossom.

**Research article:** Johnson SD. Carrion flowers. Curr Biol. 2016 Jul 11;26(13):R556-R558. doi: 10.1016/j.cub.2015.07.047. PMID: 27404246.

This book discusses the fascinating pollination strategy of the flowers from the genus *Arum* where the flies are trapped for a day: Johnson SD. Carrion flowers. Curr Biol. 2016 Jul 11;26(13):R556-R558. doi: 10.1016/j.cub.2015.07.047. PMID: 27404246.

## Ernest Gianoli and Chameleon Vines

**Vox Article: Detailed article on the unique ability of chameleon vines.** https://www.vox.com/down-to-Earth/2022/11/30/23473062/plant-mimicry-boquila-trifoliolata

**The Scientist Article: Discusses the divided opinions on the mechanism behind the mimicry of chameleon vines.** https://www.the-scientist.com/news-opinion/can-plants-see-in-the-wake-of-a-controversial-study-the-answer-is-still-unclear-70796

**Original Research Paper by Gianoli:** Gianoli E, Carrasco-Urra F. Leaf mimicry in a climbing plant protects against herbivory. Curr Biol. 2014 May 5;24(9):984-7. doi: 10.1016/j.cub.2014.03.010. Epub 2014 Apr 24. PMID: 24768053.

**Controversial Paper on the vine mimicking the plastic plant:** Jacob White & Felipe Yamashita (2022) *Boquila trifoliolata* mimics leaves of an artificial plastic host plant, Plant Signalling & Behaviour, 17:1, DOI: 10.1080/15592324.2021.1977530.

## Learning Ability and Memory Among Plants

*Mimosa pudica* **Learning Ability:** Gagliano M, Renton M, Depczynski M, Mancuso S. Experience teaches plants to learn faster and forget slower in environments where it matters. Oecologia. 2014 May;175(1):63-72. doi: 10.1007/s00442-013-2873-7. Epub 2014 Jan 5. PMID: 24390479.

**Plant Sibling Recognition: McMaster University. "Plants Recognize Their Siblings, Biologists Discover."**

ScienceDaily. ScienceDaily, 14 June 2007. <www.sciencedaily.com/releases/2007/06/070613120941.htm>.

.Intelligence Among Plants: Trewavas A. Aspects of plant intelligence. Ann Bot. 2003 Jul;92(1):1-20. doi: 10.1093/aob/mcg101. Epub 2003 May 9. PMID: 12740212; PMCID: PMC4243628.

Plant Intelligence Review: Paco Calvo, et al., Plants are intelligent, here's how. Annals of Botany, Volume 125, Issue 1, 2 January 2020, Pages 11–28, https://doi.org/10.1093/aob/mcz155.

## Planck's Principle on Scientific Shifts

Planck's principle. (2023, December 9). In Wikipedia. https://en.wikipedia.org/wiki/Planck%27s_principle.

## Penzias and Wilson Discover Cosmic Microwave Radiation

Accessed at: https://www.pbs.org/wgbh/aso/databank/entries/dp65co.html.

## Scientific Contributions of J.C. Bose

Overview Article: This article extensively covers the scientific contributions of Dr. J.C. Bose: https://www.cv.nrao.edu/~demerson/bose/bose.html.

J.C. Bose Institution Website: Additional information about Dr. Bose's scientific contributions can be found here: http://www.jcbose.ac.in/founder.

Research Paper: Highlights the role of Dr. J.C. Bose in plant neurobiology: Tandon PN. Jagdish Chandra

Bose & plant neurobiology. Indian J Med Res. 2019 May;149(5):593-599. doi: 10.4103/ijmr.IJMR_392_19. PMID: 31417026; PMCID: PMC6702694.

**Book by Bose:** Bose JC. The nervous mechanisms of plants. London: Longmans, Green and Co; 1926.

## Perkin and the Discovery of Mauve

**Book Reference:** Chronicles the scientific life of William Perkin and his discovery of Mauve. Garfield, S. (2002). Mauve: How One Man Invented a Colour That Changed the World. W. W. Norton & Company.

**Science and Industry Museum Blog:** Article on Perkin's discovery of the first synthetic dye. Accessed at: https://blog.scienceandindustrymuseum.org.uk/worlds-first-synthetic-dye/.

**Science Museum Article:** "Colourful Chemistry: Artificial Dyes." Accessed at: https://www.sciencemuseum.org.uk/objects-and-stories/chemistry/colourful-chemistry-artificial-dyes.

## Paul Ehrlich and His Scientific Contributions

**Paul Ehrlich and Chemotherapy:** Bosch F, Rosich L. "The contributions of Paul Ehrlich to pharmacology: a tribute on the occasion of the centenary of his Nobel Prize." Pharmacology. 2008;82(3):171-9. DOI: 10.1159/000149583. Epub 2008 Aug 5. PMID: 18679046; PMCID: PMC2790789.

**Ehrlich's Pioneer Work:** Androustos G. Paul Ehrlich (1854-1915): founder of chemotherapy and pioneer of haematology, immunology, and oncology. J BUON. 2004 Oct-Dec;9(4):485-91. PMID: 17415859.

## Lipitor: The Highest-Selling Drug of All Time

**Accessed at:** https://theconversation.com/weekly-dose-lipitor-the-highest-selling-drug-of-all-time-55706#:~:text=Lipitor%252520was%252520first%252520approved%252520in,US%25252412%252520billion%252520a%252520year.

## Heath Ledger's Death Due to Drug Overdose

Wikipedia Article: Detailed account of Heath Ledger's life, career, and circumstances surrounding his death. Accessed at Wikipedia.

## Drug Design and Enzyme Structure

Article on 3D Structures of Enzymes: Discusses the significance of 3D enzyme structures for drug design and rare disease therapies. Accessed at Newcastle University.

## Slowest Biological Reactions Without Enzymes

University of North Carolina School of Medicine: "Without Enzyme Catalyst, Slowest Known Biological Reaction Takes 1 Trillion Years." ScienceDaily. Accessed at ScienceDaily.

## Overdose of Painkiller and Liver Failure

Research Article: Liver injury induced by paracetamol and challenges associated with its use. Rotundo L, Pyrsopoulos N. World J Hepatol. 2020 Apr 27;12(4):125-136.

doi: 10.4254/wjh.v12.i4.125. PMID: 32685105; PMCID: PMC7336293.

### Venom-Based Painkillers

**Spider Venom:** Research on spider venom for pain relief. University of Queensland News. Accessed at University of Queensland.

**Snake Venom: Article on snake venom in painkillers.** Nature News. Accessed at Nature.

Venom in Pain Therapeutics: Trim SA, Trim CM. Venom: the sharp end of pain therapeutics. Br J Pain. 2013 Nov;7(4):179-88. doi: 10.1177/2049463713502005. PMID: 26516522; PMCID: PMC4590164.

**The evolution of snake venom:** Schendel V, Rash LD, Jenner RA, Undheim EAB. The Diversity of Venom: The Importance of Behavior and Venom System Morphology in Understanding Its Ecology and Evolution. Toxins (Basel). 2019 Nov 14;11(11):666. doi: 10.3390/toxins11110666. PMID: 31739590; PMCID: PMC6891279.

### Marsili Syndrome - A Family That Feels Almost No Pain

Smithsonian Magazine Article: Insights into the Marsili family's unique insensitivity to pain. Accessed at Smithsonian Magazine.

### The Dose Makes the Poison

Book Reference: Frank, P., & Ottoboni, M. A. The Dose Makes the Poison: A Plain-Language Guide to Toxicology. Wiley.

## Helicobacter Pylori and Duodenal Ulcer/Stomach Cancer

**Antacids Mechanisms:** Katzung, B. G. (2017). Basic and Clinical Pharmacology (14th ed.). McGraw-Hill Education.

**Interview with Barry Marshall: Insights into the discovery of H. pylori's role in ulcers. Accessed at Discover Magazine.**

**Original Research Paper regarding the discovery of *H.Pylori* among the ulcer patients:** Marshall, B. J., & Warren, J. R. (1984). "Unidentified curved bacilli in the stomach of patients with gastritis and peptic ulceration." Lancet, 1(8390), 1311-1315.

**Nobel Prize Lecture: Insights into the discovery of H. pylori. Accessed at the Nobel Prize website.**

**Biographical Information: Detailed biographies of Barry Marshall and J. Robin Warren. Accessed at the Nobel Prize Official Website.**

**In-depth Reviews:** Extensive research on *H. pylori* can be found in journals such as Gastroenterology, The American Journal of Gastroenterology, and The New England Journal of Medicine.

## Sleeping Sickness

Research Article: Kennedy PGE, Rodgers J. Clinical and Neuropathogenetic Aspects of Human African Trypanosomiasis. Front Immunol. 2019 Jan 25;10:39. doi: 10.3389/fimmu.2019.00039. PMID: 30740102; PMCID: PMC6355679.

## Viruses and Cancer

**American Cancer Society Article**: Current data on the role of viruses in causing cancer. Accessed at American Cancer Society.

**The role of viruses in causing cancer among the humans:** zur Hausen H. Viruses in human cancers. Science. 1991 Nov 22;254(5035):1167-73. doi: 10.1126/science.1659743. PMID: 1659743.

## Quotes on Science and Courage

Carl Sagan's Quote: Accessed at Goodreads.

Paul Dirac's Quote: Accessed at AZ Quotes.

## *Toxoplasma gondii* and Behavioral Manipulation

**Research on *Toxoplasma gondii*:** Abdulai-Saiku S, Tong WH, Vyas A. Behavioural Manipulation by *Toxoplasma gondii*: Does Brain Residence Matter? Trends Parasitol. 2021 May;37(5):381-390. doi: 10.1016/j.pt.2020.12.006. Epub 2021 Jan 15. PMID: 33461902.

**Dendritic Retraction in Amygdala:** Mitra R, Sapolsky RM, Vyas A. *Toxoplasma gondii* infection induces dendritic retraction in basolateral Amygdala accompanied by reduced corticosterone secretion. Dis Model Mech. 2013 Mar;6(2):516-20. doi: 10.1242/dmm.009928. Epub 2012 Oct 25. PMID: 23104989; PMCID: PMC3597033.

## *Toxoplasma gondii* and Entrepreneurial Attitudes:

**Article in the Harvard Business Review:** Research shows a link between *Toxoplasma gondii* infection and entrepreneurial behaviors. Accessed at Harvard Business Review.

**Original research article:** Johnson SK, Fitza MA, Lerner DA, Calhoun DM, Beldon MA, Chan ET, Johnson PTJ. Risky business: linking *Toxoplasma gondii* infection and entrepreneurship behaviours across individuals and countries. Proc Biol Sci. 2018 Jul 25;285(1883):20180822. doi: 10.1098/rspb.2018.0822. PMID: 30051870; PMCID: PMC6083268.

**Attraction to Cat Urine:** Faulkner, E. Fatal attraction. Nat Rev Microbiol 5, 396 (2007). https://doi.org/10.1038/nrmicro1687.

## The Discovery of Librium

Historical Article: Wick JY. The history of benzodiazepines. Consult Pharm. 2013 Sep;28(9):538-48. doi: 10.4140/TCP.n.2013.538. PMID: 24007886.

## Evolution of Taste

**Sweet Taste Preference:** Beauchamp GK. Why do we like the sweet taste: A bitter tale? Physiol Behav. 2016 Oct 1;164(Pt B):432-437. doi: 10.1016/j.physbeh.2016.05.007. Epub 2016 May 9. PMID: 27174610; PMCID: PMC5003684.

**Bitter Taste Evolution:** Callaway E. Evolutionary biology: the lost appetites. Nature. 2012 Jun 20;486(7403):S16-7. doi: 10.1038/486S16a. PMID: 22717398.

## Mechanism of Action of Antidepressants

**Mayo Clinic Article:** Overview of the mechanism of SSRIs. Accessed at Mayo Clinic.

Antidepressants Were an Accidental Discovery

Hillhouse TM, Porter JH. A brief history of the development of antidepressant drugs: from monoamines to glutamate. Exp Clin Psychopharmacol. 2015 Feb;23(1):1-21. doi: 10.1037/a0038550. PMID: 25643025; PMCID: PMC4428540.

**This paper casts doubt on the serotonin theory of depression:** Moncrieff, J., Cooper, R.E., Stockmann, T. *et al.* The serotonin theory of depression: a systematic umbrella review of the evidence. *Mol Psychiatry* 28, 3243–3256 (2023). https://doi.org/10.1038/s41380-022-01661-0

## The Role of Gut Microbiome in Diseases Including Depression

Hou, K., Wu, ZX., Chen, XY. et al. Microbiota in health and diseases. Sig Transduct Target Ther 7, 135 (2022). doi: 10.1038/s41392-022-00974-4. Accessed at Nature.

## The Role of Dopamine in Fostering Creativity

Zabelina DL, Colzato L, Beeman M, Hommel B. Dopamine and the Creative Mind: Individual Differences in Creativity Are Predicted by Interactions between Dopamine Genes DAT and COMT. PLoS One. 2016 Jan 19;11(1):e0146768. doi: 10.1371/journal.pone.0146768. PMID: 26783754; PMCID: PMC4718590.

The role of dopamine as molecule that is released in a moment of surprise and it's link with exploration and creativity:

Lieberman, Daniel Z., and Michael E. Long. The Molecule of More. BenBella Books (14 Aug. 2018)

## The Working Mechanism of Painkillers

**Working mechanism of NSAIDs:** Cashman JN. The mechanisms of action of NSAIDs in analgesia. Drugs. 1996;52 Suppl 5:13-23. doi: 10.2165/00003495-199600525-00004. PMID: 8922554.

## The Working Mechanism of Opioid Painkillers

Bovill JG. Mechanisms of actions of opioids and non-steroidal anti-inflammatory Drugs. Eur J Anaesthesiol Suppl. 1997 May;15:9-15. doi: 10.1097/00003643-199705001-00003. PMID: 9202932.

Preuss CV, Kalava A, King KC. Prescription of Controlled Substances: Benefits and Risks. [Updated 2023 Apr 29]. In: StatPearls [Internet]. Treasure Island (FL): StatPearls Publishing; 2023 Jan-. Available from: NCBI.

**Candace Pert's discovery of the opioid receptors:** Pert CB, Snyder SH. Opiate receptor: demonstration in nervous tissue. Science. 1973 Mar 9;179(4077):1011-4. doi: 10.1126/science.179.4077.1011. PMID: 4687585.

## Bill Bryson's Quote on Protons and Electrons

Bryson, B. (2003). A Short History of Nearly Everything. Broadway Books.

## The Working Mechanism of Antibiotics

**Antibiotics and their mechanism of action:** Kapoor G, Saigal S, Elongavan A. Action and resistance mechanisms of antibiotics: A guide for clinicians. J Anaesthesiol Clin Pharmacol. 2017 Jul-Sep;33(3):300-305. doi: 10.4103/joacp.JOACP_349_15. PMID: 29109626; PMCID: PMC5672523.

## History of Penicillin's Discovery

Kalb, Claudia. Spark: How Genius Ignites, from Child Prodigies to Late Bloomers. National Geographic Society, 2021.

## Data on group B Streptococcus Infection

World Health Organization: Group B Streptococcus infection causes an estimated 150,000 preventable stillbirths and infant deaths every year. Accessed at WHO.

## Alexander Fleming on Antibiotic Overuse

Rosenblatt-Farrell N. The landscape of antibiotic resistance. Environ Health Perspect. 2009 Jun;117(6):A244-50. doi: 10.1289/ehp.117-a244. PMID: 19590668; PMCID: PMC2702430.

## Bacteriophages as an Alternative to Modern Antibiotics

**Article on phage therapy:** Lin DM, Koskella B, Lin HC. Phage therapy: An alternative to antibiotics in the age of multi-Drug resistance. World J Gastrointest Pharmacol

Ther. 2017 Aug 6;8(3):162-173. doi: 10.4292/wjgpt. v8.i3.162. PMID: 28828194; PMCID: PMC5547374.

**Freethink Video:** Captures the journey of a cystic fibrosis patient who found hope in bacteriophages after antibiotics failed. Accessed at Freethink.

Keen EC. A century of phage research: bacteriophages and the shaping of modern biology. Bioessays. 2015 Jan;37(1):6-9. doi: 10.1002/bies.201400152. PMID: 25521633; PMCID: PMC4418462.

## Quorum Sensing and Antibiotic Resistance

Zhao X, Yu Z, Ding T. Quorum Sensing Regulation of Antimicrobial Resistance in Bacteria. Microorganisms. 2020 Mar 17;8(3):425. doi: 10.3390/ microorganisms8030425. PMID: 32192182; PMCID: PMC7143945.

## Mechanism of Action of Contraceptives

Rivera R, Yacobson I, Grimes D. The mechanism of action of hormonal contraceptives and intrauterine contraceptive devices. Am J Obstet Gynecol. 1999 Nov;181(5 Pt 1):1263-9. doi: 10.1016/s0002-9378(99)70120-1. PMID: 10561657.

## Embryonic Diapause

Fenelon JC, Banerjee A, Murphy BD. Embryonic diapause: development on hold. Int J Dev Biol. 2014;58(2-4):163-74. doi: 10.1387/ijdb.140074bm. PMID: 25023682.

## The Story of Dr. Subhas Mukherjee

**The Better India Article:** Detailed account of Dr. Subhas Mukherjee's pioneering work in IVF in India. Accessed at The Better India.

**The Print Article:** Chronicles the challenges faced by Dr. Mukherjee. Accessed at The Print.

**Detailed PDF:** Covers the scientific and personal life of Dr. Mukherjee. Accessed at NIRRCH.

## The Story of Krish Gopalakrishnan and Julio Iglesias

**Forbes Article:** Discusses Krish Gopalakrishnan's unexpected path to success. Accessed at Forbes India.

**Zen Garden Article:** Explores how Kris Gopalakrishnan's success was found on an unplanned path. Accessed at Forbes India.

**Careers360 Article:** Describes obstacles and success stories of Kris Gopalakrishnan and Julio Iglesias. Accessed at Careers360.

## John Dewey's Quote on Education

**John Dewey Quote:** "Education is not preparation for life; education is life itself." Accessed at BrainyQuote.

## Anna Sewell's Quote

**Anna Sewell Quote:** "Do your best, And leave the rest, 'Twill all come right Some day or night." Accessed at QuoteFancy.

**Image credits:**

Image 1: An artist on Fiverr was hired to create these images.

Image 2: An artist on Fiverr was hired to create these images.

Image 3: An artist on Fiverr was hired to create these images.

Image 4: An artist on Fiverr was hired to create these images.

Image 5: An artist on Fiverr was hired to create these images.

Image 6: An artist on Fiverr was hired to create these images.

Image 7: Sofian *Rafflesia*, CC BY-SA 4.0 <https://creativecommons.org/licenses/by-sa/4.0>, via Wikimedia Commons

Image 8: The image was catalogued by NASA and has been added to the public domain. The below is the description:

## ECHO Horn Antenna

The Horn reflector antenna at Bell Telephone Laboratories in Holmdel, New Jersey was built in 1959 for pioneering work in communication satellites for the NASA ECHO I. The antenna was 50 feet in length and the entire structure weighed about 18 tonnes. It was comprised of aluminium with a steel base. It was used to detect radio waves that bounced off Project ECHO balloon satellites. The horn was later modified to work with the Telstar Communication

Satellite frequencies as a receiver for broadcast signals from the satellite. In 1990 the horn was dedicated to the National Park Service as a National Historic Landmark.

Image Number: 62-Tels-20

Date: June 1961

Link: https://www.flickr.com/photos/ nasacommons/16315677368/in/photolist-qRL7sd

Image 9: The Birth Centenary Committee, printed by P.C. Ray, Public domain, via Wikimedia Commons

Image 10: Official photographer, Public domain, via Wikimedia Commons

Link: https://commons.wikimedia.org/wiki/ File:Synthetic_Production_of_Penicillin_TR1468.jpg

Image 11: Eric Koch for Anefo, CC0, via Wikimedia Commons

Image 12: **This image was created using Stability AI.**

www.ingramcontent.com/pod-product-compliance
Lightning Source LLC
Chambersburg PA
CBHW031632170726
47990CB00017B/503